The Farewell Kid

ALSO BY BARBARA WERSBA

For Young Adults

Wonderful Me
Just Be Gorgeous
Beautiful Losers
Love Is the Crooked Thing
Fat: A Love Story
Crazy Vanilla
The Carnival in My Mind
Tunes for a Small Harmonica

For Younger Readers

Twenty-Six Starlings Will Fly Through Your Mind
The Crystal Child

A novel by

BARBARA WERSBA

The Farewell Kid

HARPER & ROW, PUBLISHERS, NEW YORK
Grand Rapids, Philadelphia, St. Louis, San Francisco
London, Singapore, Sydney, Tokyo, Toronto

Typography by Joyce Hopkins
1 2 3 4 5 6 7 8 9 10
First Edition

Library of Congress Cataloging-in-Publication Data
Wersba, Barbara.
    The farewell kid: a novel / by Barbara Wersba.
        p.   cm.
    "A Charlotte Zolotow book."
    Summary: Seventeen-year-old Heidi Rosenbloom
decides against college when she finishes high school and
to devote herself to stray dogs instead; but the entrance of
photographer Harvey Beaumont into her life adds another
dimension.
    ISBN 0-06-026378-4 : $. — ISBN 0-06-026379-2
(lib. bdg.) : $
    [1. Dogs—Fiction.   2. New York (N.Y.)—Fiction.]
I. Title.
PZ7.W473Far 1990   89-36401
[Fic]—dc20   CIP
                                                 AC

The
Farewell
Kid

1

It was the year I swore off men, and the year I decided not to go to college. It was the year that my mother went to Europe with her best friend Bobo Lewis, and the year when I realized that my true mission in life was to save every stray dog in New York. In other words, it was the most important year of my life, and its hallmark was that I was saying good-bye to everything. Good-bye to the male species, who had caused me nothing but pain, and good-bye to adolescence—which had been like a long illness—and good-bye to living on Manhattan's Upper East Side. I was seventeen and a half and putting my old life behind me in every possible way. I was getting good at the word "farewell."

My name is Heidi Rosenbloom, and a great beauty I am not. What I mean is, what you get when you look at me is a short plump teenager who wears her curly hair in a crew cut and who has a voice like Woody Allen's. My nose is too big, my eyes are too small, and I am not graceful on my feet.

Repeat—I am not beautiful. And neither am I a brain. The trouble is, the person I *am* has always caused my parents a lot of grief. What my mother wanted was a daughter who would become a model or a movie star. Some kind of celebrity. And what my father had envisioned was a scholar—a girl who would go to Radcliffe and major in physics or something. A girl who would graduate *cum laude* and go on to a brilliant career.

So what had they gotten instead? Me, Heidi, a kid who bought her clothes at thrift shops and whose only passion in life was dogs. All kinds of dogs, the large and the small, the normal and the crazy, the pedigreed and the mutt. Dogs were the only people I related to, so to speak. Dogs were the only creatures who made me feel sane. Look at it this way. Most people identify with other people. But when I am with other people I feel like a foreigner—someone who doesn't understand the language or the street signs.

I have two dogs of my own—a stray named Happy, who is part Cairn and part Norfolk, and a Scottie named MacGregor who was a neglected dog who used to be part of my dog-walking group. His owner didn't want him and gave him to me. And, despite the fact that my mother protested, I kept him. God. I would have had twenty dogs if she had allowed it. But Shirley Rosenbloom is one of those people who has a neurosis about cleanliness. One dirty ashtray in the living room is enough to give her a nervous breakdown. Much less dog toys lying around. Leather chew bones.

My parents are divorced, and have been since I was thirteen. My dad lives down in Greenwich Village, and Mom lives in the big apartment on East 82nd Street. They did not have what is called a friendly divorce. No. What they had was a minor version of World War Three, with accusations and lawyers and fights over alimony. And all because of a horse's ass named Jane Anne Mosley. Yep, my father left my mother for dear old Jane Anne, age twenty-four, and then a few years later she left him. Jane Anne, I mean. But by then too many bitter things had been said and my parents could not get back together. It was sad, because I think they would have liked to marry again, but there was too much resentment in the air. So Daddy moved into his tiny apartment in the Village, and he and Mom continued to communicate over the phone. He would come up to the apartment sometimes, for birthdays and holidays, but it never really worked out.

My father owns a jewelry business on West 47th Street and is the epitome of the self-made American man. Rags to riches. My mother, on the other hand, comes from Larchmont, in Westchester, and grew up in comfort. *Her* mother, Rosalie Kantor, had a lot of money and so Mom always had the best of everything — and has tried to give me the best of everything too. Except that I do not want it. Sorry folks, but fancy prep schools and clothes from Saks Fifth Avenue are not my thing. Nor is having my hair streaked at Elizabeth Arden's my thing, or going to tea at the Plaza Hotel. Poor Shirley. She would sometimes look at me as though she thought she had been given the wrong baby in the hospital. She would look at me with a combination of love and sadness, and frustration, and genuine rage.

But it was *my* life, right? Not theirs, and not my relatives', but mine — and I was determined to make the most of it. Which is why, during the spring of my senior year at The Spencer School, on 86th Street, I was saying all those farewells.

Good-bye to luxury apartments on the East Side, and pompous doormen with names like Sylvester, and good-bye to my mother trying to improve my figure and my haircut and my clothes. Good-bye to a long string of maids, whom my mother could never keep because she was so fussy, and good-bye to Mom's massage therapist, Gladys. A special good-bye to Spencer, where I had gone since the seventh grade, and an extra-special good-bye to all my snobby classmates who were going off to college. Good-bye to higher education and good-bye to Making It. God! When people say they're going to make it, I don't even know what they're talking about. Because my life has always been filled with people—like my father—who made it, and then fell apart. Does driving a big car make you a big man? Does having power mean you are really powerful? Do money and power and possessions indicate the kind of person you are? No. *My* plans were to live in colorful poverty in a loft somewhere, with my dogs Happy and MacGregor, and devote my life to strays. During the past year I had considered becoming a groomer or a handler, or a vet's assistant—but then, one day during my senior year at Spencer, all my ideas changed.

It was a misty October morning, and I was hurriedly walking my dog-walking group in Central Park before school. I had taken over this group of dogs from Peter Applebaum, who was in my class, but whose summer vacation in Europe had slid over into a fall vacation. In other words, Peter was still in the French Alps, and I still had his group, or the Gang of Seven, as I called them. My job was to walk all of them, plus my own two dogs, in the Park twice a day—somehow managing to attend school in between—and for this I was being paid seventy dollars a day. Or, four hundred and ninety dollars a week. Which is not exactly small potatoes.

If you don't come from a big city, you probably aren't familiar with professional dog walkers—but there are a lot of them in New York, people who walk other people's dogs and make quite a bit of money. Which is the thing that struck me as being so ironic. My dad was obsessed with me earning good money, but now that I was earning it, he wasn't pleased. "What do you want to be when you're forty?" he had once shouted at me. "A professional dog walker?" And I, of course, had said yes.

I mean, why *not* walk dogs for the rest of my life, rather than spend my days sitting in an office? I did not intend to get married for a long time—if ever—and dog walking, at least, took place out of doors and was healthy. Each client paid me ten dollars a day and that was pretty good dough. So much for becoming an executive secretary. Or a dental assistant.

Anyway, it was seven in the morning and I was walking my group in the Park, near the 79th Street entrance. It was misty and cool, and the trees were just starting to turn color, and I wasn't quite awake. All of my charges lived between the 60's and the 80's on the East Side, but it really took some doing to pick all of them up, walk them, return them to their various doormen, and then get to school on time. So there we were, me, Happy, MacGregor, and the Gang of Seven, when two strays ran past us.

They were both German Shepherds, and they were skin and bones. I mean, I knew, just from one glance, that those dogs had been on the run for a long time and that they were starving. Two young German Shepherds on their own in the Park, evading the cops and living on whatever garbage they could find. There are hundreds of such dogs in New York, and most of them never receive any help. They just run in packs and scare the hell out of people. Not me, of course. All I felt was grief as they ran past. And regret—that I was burdened with so many dogs on leashes. Otherwise, I would have gone after them.

And then it hit me. What in the name of God was I doing walking people's pampered pedigreed dogs, when the dogs who *needed* me were strays. Dogs like those two young Shepherds. Dogs like Happy and MacGregor. The thing that I was meant to do—that I was born to do—was to form an organization devoted to the rescue of stray dogs. I would call it Dog Rescue, Incorporated, and run it out of my own apartment.

9

All of this came to me in a flash. No thought, no premeditation, just a flash of insight. Some people reach the age of thirty without finding what they are meant to do in this world—but I, Heidi Rosenbloom, age seventeen, had just found it. My *raison d'être*. My purpose in living.

"Wow," I said aloud. And then I sank down on a Park bench. "Sit," I said absently to my nine charges, and—for a change—they all sat down. Happy, MacGregor, a Dachshund, a Wolfhound, a Bulldog, a Poodle, a Spaniel, a Boxer, and a Dalmatian.

Suddenly my whole life was passing before my eyes—and what I saw was a person who, when little, had brought home stray dogs and cats, stray puppies and kittens—and even a stray parakeet once—only to be scolded furiously by her mother. What I saw was a kid who would weep if a houseplant was thrown out, a kid who hated to watch the TV news because it showed so many tragedies. Sit down to dinner in front of the TV and what are you presented with? The collapse of bridges, politicians committing suicide, kidnapped babies, people dying of AIDS, the destruction of the environment and imminent global war. . . . "You're too *sensitive*," I had been told all of my life, and it was true. Things—cruel things—hurt me terribly, and I had once been caught weeping over a mouse who had drowned in my mother's toilet bowl. It was Gladys, my mother's massage therapist, who had discovered me there, and she had shaken her head sadly. "Heidi, sweetheart," she said, "it was only a mouse. And it was probably his time. We all have a time to go."

Well, maybe. But the image of that mouse floating in the toilet bowl had haunted me for two years, and I had even dreamt about it a few times. Yes, I was sensitive to such things, and sensitive I would remain. I would devote my life to rescuing New York City's strays—so that someday, when I died, I would not feel that I hadn't lived. To me, that would be the most terrible fate of all—to grow old, and lie on your deathbed, and feel that you had not had your life.

This realization came to me in about one minute. I could still see those two Shepherds, disappearing over a hill somewhere in the distance, and it was starting to rain. Mentally, I thanked those poor dogs and wished them well. Because they had given me my future.

2

Before I continue with the story of me, and Dog Rescue, Incorporated—and how I met an amazing person called Harvey Beaumont the Third—I want to tell you a few more things about my life. The full significance of my leaving home that June, right after graduation, won't mean much to you unless I tell you about my troubled past.

To begin with, my mother had been informed that she could never bear a child. So that when she got pregnant, at age thirty, it was a cause for rejoicing. She spent most of her pregnancy in bed, and then what did she get? *Me*. A fat, ugly baby who cried too much. A sullen baby, who was spoiled rotten and sent to a progressive nursery school where classical music was played softly during nap hours. Then on to The Howard Grammar School—a posh institution on East 63rd Street—and finally on to Spencer.

The point is that Shirley adored me. Maybe if she had had other children, it wouldn't have been so bad — but from the day I made my entrance into the world, she treated me like the heir apparent. Like someone who had to be groomed and polished in anticipation of a royal job. Handmade dresses, and an English nanny, and toys from F.A.O. Schwarz, and piano teachers with names like Gilda Landauer.

The best of everything . . . but I didn't want it. All I wanted, as I became eight, and nine, and ten, was to own a dog and ride my three-speed bike in Central Park. All I wanted was to skulk around New York in old jeans and sneakers, and sit in movies — sometimes seeing the same movie three times — and read the dog stories of James Herriott. All of which my mother tolerated. But then, when I hit puberty, she lost patience. It was as though she had been biding her time for twelve long years in anticipation of the day when she could start taking me to beauty parlors and hairdressers and boutiques. It was as though my childhood had been a holding pattern, which was now breaking up into what she hoped would be a whirlwind of feminine activity.

Who did she really want for a daughter? Brooke Shields. Or, to go back a few generations, June Allyson. Or maybe Miss America. The Miss America Pageant was one of my mother's favorite shows on television, and when the winner would get

13

crowned, Shirley would always cry. The tall, gorgeous—and seemingly lobotomized—winner would walk down the runway with a bouquet of roses in her arms, and Shirley Rosenbloom would weep—imagining her own little Heidi on that runway, her own flesh and blood. *Therefore.* When I began to resist the beauty parlors and hairdressers, the boutiques and specialty shops and department stores, all hell broke loose. In other words, Shirley and I began to fight.

We fought about my boys' clothes and we fought about my crew cut. We fought over the fact that I wanted to decorate my room *my* way instead of hers, and we fought over my friends, or lack of them. We fought and yelled at each other, and retired to our separate bedrooms to weep, and then it would start all over again. World War Four. The clash of the planets.

During my junior year at Spencer, she suddenly gave in. It was as though I had finally worn her down, because we came to a truce. She would let me dress the way I liked as long as I walked down the back stairs of our building instead of using the elevator. She would let me decorate my room my way, and she would let me keep the two dogs. Maybe she thought I was about to run away. But happy about the situation, she was not.

All of which was exacerbated, if that is the word, when I told her that I would not be going to college. I mean, that was the last straw in her very small haystack. I, Heidi, Miss New York Prep School, was refusing to go to college. What I intended to do instead, I told her, was strike out on my own.

"Strike out on your own!" she exclaimed. "And what does that mean?"

"I have six thousand dollars in the bank," I said. "In checking."

"Six thousand? And how long do you think that will last, Heidi? Six thousand is pennies."

As usual, Shirley was wearing her peach satin robe and three strands of pearls. Her hair was in rollers, in preparation for a cocktail party she was attending that afternoon, and she smelled of Chanel No. 5. My mother has always reminded me of the actress Joan Bennett in old movies on television. She is small and dark and pretty. And very theatrical.

She was pacing the living room—our living room that is crowded with antiques, and a piano, and two couches, and paintings, and objets d'art—and she looked distraught. We had had this conversation before, but now it was getting serious.

"What will people say if we don't send you to college?" she said to me. "What will people think?"

"People? Which people?"

"Every friend I have has a child in college!"

"So we can't be different, right?"

"There is still time for you to apply to Hunter. Your guidance counselor said so."

"Sorry, Mom. No way."

"You have no gratitude!" she cried. "The best of everything, and you're not grateful. Your father has *slaved* to give you the best in life, only to hear that you want to work with dogs. Dogs! Why not sheep or horses? Why not cows?"

"You're not being fair."

Shirley looked like she was about to cry. "Ah, what's the use? We gave you everything, and now you tell us you don't want it."

She sank down on her small antique love seat and pressed her hands to her eyes — a gesture straight out of the soap operas she watches every day. Her distress over my proposed lack of a college education was funny, when you came right down to it, because *she* wasn't educated at all. After high school, she had attended a school of interior design for one year, and then she had married Leonard.

My father had no education either — but for him, my situation had a different meaning because Leonard is a frustrated intellectual. Which is why he fell in love with Jane Anne — a writer who had published a story in *The New Yorker*. I had visited the two of them once, at her Village apartment, and it was all books and no furniture, and obscure music on the stereo. Poor Daddy. He really thought Jane Anne was the cat's meow because she took him to outdoor concerts and off-Broadway plays.

My gut instinct told me that Shirley and Leonard wanted me to be educated for their sakes — not mine. Wanted to be able to tell people that their daughter went to Radcliffe. Wanted to drive up, for the weekend, to some verdant campus where clean-cut kids were carrying their books across the lawn, and where one took one's parents to the campus coffee shop for a soda.

It was autumn when we had this conversation — so that by spring, Shirley had begun to accept the fact that I really was not going to college. As for Leonard, he had stated, quite simply, that I had broken his heart. What's more, he said, there would be no funds emanating from him. No more allowance and no more handouts of ten and twenty bucks at a time. "You want to strike out on your own," he told me, "fine. But no more handouts from the old man. See what it's like out there, Heidi, and then come back and we'll talk."

What he meant, of course, was the world. Go out into the world and see what it's like. But I felt fine about the world already — and by spring I was secretly going through my possessions, deciding which things to take with me and which to abandon, and I was also reading the real estate pages of *The New York Times.*

What I had hoped for was a loft down in SoHo, or an interesting apartment in the East Village. But the rents were fantastic. Lofts were renting for three thousand dollars a month, and flats in the East Village—on crummy streets—were priced at six and seven hundred. Wow, I said to myself, this is not going to be easy.

Meanwhile, I dragged myself through my last months at Spencer, doing no studying at all, and composing ads for Dog Rescue, Incorporated.

"Dog Rescue, Incorporated:" I wrote. "A new concept in the humane treatment of animals. If you have lost a dog, we will find him. If you wish to adopt a dog, we will provide one. Our aim is to banish the word *stray.*"

And then, on June 3rd, I graduated from The Spencer School, where I had gone since the seventh grade. Yep, I stood up there on the platform, in a hideous white dress, and sang the school anthem along with everyone else. Many of my classmates had tears in their eyes—at the thought of leaving dear old Spencer—but the only thing I felt was relief. And a kind of secret joy. For six years I had been an outcast at this school—a member of no group, no clique—and when my one and only friend Veronica moved to Los Angeles, I had been completely alone. But now I was about to be liberated from this prison and my heart was pounding with joy. Meanwhile, in the auditorium below, Shirley and Leonard were sitting together in a rare show of unanimity—watching their only child graduate from the most expensive prep school in New York.

3

"It's a stroke of luck," I said to Veronica over the phone. "A complete stroke of luck. With Mother and Bobo away, I can find an apartment and move out of here."

"You mean, you'd move without telling Shirley?" Veronica asked. "What happens when she gets back and finds you gone?"

"I'll deal with that when it happens. But you've got to admit that it's a stroke of luck."

The thing I was talking about, long-distance, was the fact that my mother and Bobo were going to Europe for three weeks. The trip was supposed to be my graduation present from Bobo, but when I refused to go, she had decided to just take Shirley. Bobo had envisioned the three of us on this journey—so there was a bit of resentment in the air. But God! I just couldn't see myself barreling through Europe with Mom and Bobo Lewis. . . . Bobo is a big fat cheerful woman—a rich widow—who is kind at heart, but somewhat vulgar. She lives in

Westchester in a small mansion, and has a butler and everything, and she was taking Mom to Paris on the Concorde. Five countries in three weeks was their plan, and I could *not* see myself participating. They would stay in first-class hotels and rent private cars. They were going to visit a friend of Bobo's who lives on the Riviera.

"What did Leonard and Shirley give you?" Veronica was asking. "For graduation, I mean."

"Leonard bought me some IBM stock, which he says I can't have until I'm twenty-one—and Shirley gave me her little diamond earrings. Just what I always wear. Diamonds."

"Right, right," said Veronica sympathetically. "But look—*my* mom gave me pearls for graduation. And where, I ask you, would I wear pearls? I'm either in a bathing suit or a pair of shorts. You know what L.A. is like."

Actually, I didn't know what L.A. was like, but I didn't feel like saying so. "At any rate," I said, "it's my big chance. By the time they get back from Europe, I'll have my own apartment."

"You're brave, not going to college. If I hadn't agreed to go to UCLA, I think my mom would have murdered me."

"I'm marching to a different drummer," I said. "I always have."

21

After we hung up, I realized that what I had said to Veronica was true. I had always marched to a different drummer, only I hadn't known it until recently. And the sound of this drummer was not like anyone else's. It was hard to be as different as I was, but it was also exciting. Because there were all those possibilities out there, in the world. All those potentials.

I sat down on my bed, on which my two dogs were sleeping, and looked at my room. Soon it would be empty of possessions, just another spare room in Shirley's apartment. It was June 6th, and in one week Shirley and Bobo would depart.

As though my thoughts had swept her into the room, Shirley barged in without knocking. Sometimes she knocks, and sometimes she doesn't. It's a barometer of her state of mind.

"I've just been talking on the phone to Bobo," she said, "and she says that there is still time for you to change your mind. She hasn't cancelled your plane ticket. You can still come."

She looked around for someplace to sit, and finally chose a piano bench I had found abandoned on Third Avenue. It was a heavy bench, made of mahogany, and I had brought it home in a cab. "You can still change your mind," she repeated.

She gazed at my room and sighed. Until recently,

this room had been a young girl's boudoir of pink and blue, all ruffles and chintz. Now it was a utilitarian place, filled with "found objects," and my collection of dog books, and Happy and MacGregor's possessions. Collars, leashes, dog bowls and toys. "God," she said to herself. "This room."

There was silence for a moment, and then Shirley returned to the subject at hand. "So shall I call Bobo back, or what? She hasn't cancelled your ticket."

"Mom," I said patiently, "I'm not going. I'm sorry to disappoint you, but I do not want to go to Europe this summer. And especially not with Bobo."

That one, of course, made her furious. "Not with Bobo? Well, let me tell you something, miss. You could do a lot worse. How many girls get offered a trip to Europe when they are only seventeen? Any other girl would be thrilled."

"I am not any other girl. I'm me."

"Out of the kindness of her heart, Bobo offers you a trip, first class all the way, and you turn her down. She was shocked. And very hurt, believe me."

All of a sudden, I felt exhausted. "Mom, please. I don't want to go. I wouldn't have a good time."

"We'll be on the Riviera for four whole days."

"Mom . . ."

"England, France, Switzerland—another girl would jump at the chance. But not you, oh no, not Heidi."

She pulled her satin robe more tightly about her and stared at Happy and MacGregor, who were snoring away on the bed. "It smells of dog in here."

Don't worry, I said silently. Because very soon, it won't smell of dog at all. Soon, you can return this place to its former beauty. Pink and blue, ruffles and chintz. A glass dressing table with perfume bottles on it. French flower prints on the wall.

"Well, all right," said Shirley, "we'll go without you. But it will be a long time, I assure you, before Bobo will do anything for you again. You hurt her very much, Heidi. She was crushed."

I tried to imagine Bobo being crushed. It would be like crushing an elephant.

"She'll recover," I said.

A hard look crossed my mother's face. "If you think I'm not keeping tabs on you while we're away, you're wrong. I will phone you twice a week, and your father will be in touch daily. I will not have you running wild when I'm gone."

"When have I ever run wild?"

"What you will *do* for three weeks here alone, I can't imagine."

"I'll survive."

24

She gave me an angry look, and then she looked away. And for a moment, I just wanted to go over and hug her and put everything right. It was so confusing—because there were some years when we were friends, and some years when we were enemies. What we were right now, I didn't know, but it did not feel comfortable.

To make a long story short, my mother spent the next week shopping, and getting a permanent, and packing, and repacking. And on the afternoon of June 12th, Bobo showed up in her Cadillac, with the butler driving, to take herself and Shirley to the airport. Bobo had seven pieces of luggage with her and was dressed in a red silk suit that made her look huge. Her strawberry blond hair was more strawberry—and more blond—than ever. She did not look crushed.

I hugged Bobo and then I hugged my mother, who, very briefly, began to cry. "Now don't forget," she said to me, "I'm phoning you every Tuesday and Friday. Ten A.M., your time."

"Good-bye," I said, my voice wavering a little. Because I knew that by the time they returned, I would be living a different life. Yes, by then, I, Heidi Rosenbloom, would be ensconced in her own apartment and running her own business. Dog Rescue, Incorporated.

4

Find an apartment? I must have been crazy—
because it was soon apparent that there *were* no
apartments in New York. At least, none that I could
afford. With Happy and MacGregor in tow, and
with *The New York Times* under my arm, I trudged
from building to building. A studio apartment on
East 22nd Street cost nine hundred dollars a month.
A two-bedroom in the West Village cost twenty-
five hundred. In Chinatown, I saw an "attractive
one-bedroom walkup" for eight hundred dollars.
On West 165th Street there was something that
resembled a large closet—with a bathroom—for five
seventy-five.

And then there were the dogs. I mean, the minute
the person who was showing me an apartment saw
Happy and MacGregor, he or she demurred. God,
I thought, what if they knew that I intended to house
lots of dogs? How am I going to get away with
this?

I looked at apartments for three days—from nine

to five — and saw not one that I could afford. I covered whole neighborhoods, and sat drinking coffee in restaurants — and eventually I just left Happy and MacGregor at home, because they were so bored by the whole thing. By the fourth day, I have to admit to you, I was getting very discouraged. But then I met The Man In Gray.

He was everywhere I went that afternoon. If I was looking at a flat on East 14th Street, he was too. And if I was trudging up the steps of a brownstone on East 10th, he was one step behind me. We kept bumping into each other, and doing things in tandem, until finally he confronted me. "My name is Chester Gilroy," he said, extending his hand. "I guess we should introduce ourselves."

We were standing outside of a loft building on East 15th and there was a light rain falling. "I'm Heidi Rosenbloom," I said, shaking his hand. "Hi."

He was around thirty, and he was wearing a very expensive-looking gray suit. A dark tie. Polished shoes. A briefcase under his arm. "May I buy you a cup of coffee?" he asked. "You must be as tired as I am."

He seemed pleasant enough, a sort of junior executive type, so I let him take me to a coffee shop on First Avenue. Very few people in this world try to pick me up, so I was flattered. And a person named Chester Gilroy, I reasoned, was probably safe. It was too bad I was wearing a pair of jeans and a T-shirt, but what the hell. This was a chance meeting.

"It's murder, isn't it?" he said, as we sat down at a table in Hildy's Coffee Shop. "I've been looking for months."

"Months?" I replied. "Is it that hard to find an apartment?"

He gave me a weary look. "I've been pounding the pavement for three months, and there's still nothing I can afford. I even took a course to prepare myself for this ordeal. Down at The School of Contemporary Thought. On 12th Street."

"A course? In finding an apartment?"

"Absolutely. It's called *Finding an Apartment: The Hidden Market*, and I must say, it was invaluable. Not that I've found one yet. But they do give you pointers."

Our coffee arrived, and I poured milk into mine. "Like what?"

Chester Gilroy loosened his tie and tapped a small package of artificial sweetener into his coffee. "Well, first of all, they advise you to concentrate on neighborhoods, not just individual apartments. Work the neighborhood, so to speak. Get to know the shopkeepers and doormen and supers. Talk to

28

people who are moving their cars from one side of the street to the other. Do *mailings*. I have a friend who did five mailings in two months, and she finally came up with something. A nice clean studio apartment on Horatio Street. She had to pay Key Money, of course, which is the bribe you pay to get anything these days, but it was worth it."

"How much did she have to pay?"

Chester finished his coffee and took out a cigarette. "Five thousand to the rental agent. But the apartment is only five hundred a month."

I gave a long whistle through my teeth and sat there, considering this information. "Wow," I said, "this is tougher than I thought."

Chester was perusing me, but not in an unfriendly way. "If you don't mind my saying so, you look rather young to be renting an apartment."

I gave him a cool look. "I'm twenty-five."

He laughed nervously. "Sorry. How much can you pay?"

"Five hundred a month, maybe. But I need a big place. I have—or will have—a lot of dogs."

He shook his head. "Dogs are definitely a drawback. My friend who got the apartment on Horatio Street has a dog, but it's a Chihuahua. Tiny. She kept him in her bag while she looked at the place. No one knew a thing."

"Well, I'm sorry, but I will have a few dogs with me. I'm going into the dog rescue business."

Chester blew a stream of smoke into the air. "It sounds like you need commercial space. But that's even more expensive than residential. Aha, I've got it! I've just thought of something."

I leaned forward. "What?"

"Two days ago I saw some commercial space on East 81st Street. An old barbershop. Four hundred a month."

"Four hundred? Wow. How come?"

"Because the building is going to be demolished in eight months, and most of the apartments above the shop are empty. The super won't *tell* you that, of course. He'll just say that some renovation is going on. But I got the scoop from the Chinese laundryman next door."

"Gee. That's a real possibility."

Chester took out his business card and started to write on it. "Here's the address, and the name of the super is Montaldo. A very sneaky type and not to be trusted. What I advise is that you slip him twenty before the negotiations start."

"Would he give me a lease?"

"Of course not. It's all under the table."

We rose to our feet and stood there looking at each other. We had only been acquainted for a half hour, but I felt like he was a relative or some-thing. Uncle Chester.

"Chester," I said, "you've been wonderful. I really appreciate it."

He smiled at me. "It was my pleasure."

"If I get the barbershop, I'll phone you."

He straightened his tie and ran one hand through his short black hair. "I've got to be going now. I'm seeing a sublet up on Riverside Drive."

"Au revoir," I said.

After he was gone, I took a closer look at his business card. It said, "Gilroy Enterprises." And then, just a phone number.

Wondering what Chester's enterprises could be, I stepped out onto First Avenue, hailed a cab, and gave the driver the address on 81st Street. When we arrived, I saw that the building was a shabby brownstone with a barbershop on the first floor and five stories above. Most of the upper windows had boards across them.

I stepped into the entryway, rang the buzzer that said "Super," and almost at once Mr. Montaldo came down the stairs. He was very handsome, but not to be trusted, I decided—and before he could open his mouth, I handed him a twenty-dollar bill. "I'm interested in renting the barbershop," I said. "My name is Rosenbloom."

5

Ernesto Montaldo took a ring of keys from his belt and unlocked the door of the shop, which fronted the sidewalk. There was still a striped pole outside the door, and a sign that said, "Bruce's Barbershop." Together, Mr. Montaldo and I stepped into the darkness.

"Let me get on some lights," he said. "What we need is lights."

He moved towards the back of the shop, found the lights, and flicked them on. Suddenly, the place was illuminated—and what I saw was a big room with mirrors along one wall and eight barber chairs in a row. And that was all. Just a room with some barber's chairs and a couple of white porcelain sinks. "You mean, this is *it*?" I said to Montaldo.

"No, no, no," he said quickly. "There's more, in the back. A lovely toilet and shower. A very good kitchen."

He led me into the rear of the shop, where there was a small bathroom and a makeshift kitchen that held a table, a hot plate, and a refrigerator. Everything was filthy. But the space was not bad. In fact, if I could just remove the barber chairs out front the space would be excellent. "Is there heat?" I asked.

Montaldo nodded vigorously. "Oh yes. Steam heat. Wonderful in winter."

"Would there be any way to remove the barber chairs?"

His face fell. "Oh no, I don't think so. They are cemented into the floor."

I walked back into the front room, wondering where I could put a bed, a bureau, a desk. "I don't know. . . ."

"Look," said Montaldo, "the rent for this is four hundred a month. But for *you*, we make an exception. For *you*, the rent would be three fifty. And there is no such rent as three fifty in the whole city of New York. You know that, miss. You must be aware."

"Well . . ."

"Three fifty a month, in cash, to me, and no questions asked. Good heat in the winter. And we take children and pets."

I stared at him. "You do?"

"Children, dogs, cats, anything. The man upstairs, on the second floor, has a ferret. You know what that is, a ferret?"

"Sure."

"He keeps a ferret and no questions asked. He is the only other tenant because we are renovating at the moment. Mr. Morganthau."

"I'll take it," I said. "Do you want me to sign anything?"

Montaldo shook his head. "Signing is not necessary. But we *do* ask for two months' security, and the first month's rent. In cash, of course."

I did some quick mathematics in my head. "Let me go to the bank and get the money. I'll be back in an hour."

Montaldo smiled. "And then, there is the little matter of the super's fee."

"Super's fee?"

"What we ask of you is perhaps fifty dollars."

I sighed. "OK. But I'll have to go to the bank. Will you promise not to rent this place to anyone else while I'm gone?"

He extended his hand. "You have my word, miss. And the word of a Montaldo is like writing in blood."

I winced, and shook his hand. "Right. I'll be back in thirty minutes."

As soon as I left the shop and started to walk towards the bank on Lexington, where my savings are, I realized something awful. And this was the fact that the barbershop was exactly three blocks from my mother's apartment. Shirley's apartment was on 82nd Street off Lexington, and this was on 81st Street off Second Avenue. An unfortunate proximity. And yet, where else would I ever find such a large room for three hundred fifty a month? It might be possible to remove the barber chairs, and once I did some heavy cleaning, the place would be all right. A little dark, with just those front windows, but satisfactory.

To make a long story short, I went to the bank, withdrew eleven hundred dollars, hurried back to the barbershop and gave Montaldo the cash. In return, he gave me the key to the shop, showed me where I could plug in a phone, and hotfooted it out of there. And suddenly, I felt very excited. So what if it was only a barbershop with eight chairs and two porcelain sinks? It was *mine*.

During the next few days, I vacuumed and scrubbed the barbershop to within an inch of its life, and then I hired a mover with a small van to move my stuff. Albert, one of our doormen, started asking me questions about this, but I silenced him by saying that Shirley was simply getting rid of some furniture. It was going to relatives, upstate.

On June 19th, Happy and MacGregor and I took up residence in the barbershop. The dogs loved the place, because the room was long and great for running, and of course I had brought all their stuff with me. I had also brought my books, a bed, a bureau and a desk—all of which I placed along the one free wall of the shop. In the kitchen cubicle, I installed a new hot plate and some dime-store dishes. The only other pieces of furniture were my mahogany piano bench and a wooden chair. To cover the front windows of the shop, I used wide bamboo blinds. The floors, when scrubbed, revealed themselves to be made of black and white tile. The last thing I bought were two lamps, at the thrift shop, and a few cooking pots. But my God, how much money I had spent in just a few days! Maybe Shirley was right and six thousand wasn't a fortune. I had already spent two thousand of it.

I do have to admit that my first night in the barbershop was strange. I mean, if Happy and MacGregor hadn't been there with me, chasing their toys up and down the length of the room, I might have felt a little odd. I'd made up my bed with fresh sheets, and arranged my books in a small bookcase, and I'd brought in a Chinese dinner, but the whole thing did feel funny. No television set. No one to talk to.

I had opened an account with New York Telephone, and installed a phone in the kitchen—so I decided to call Chester Gilroy, but he wasn't home. Then I tried Veronica in L.A., but she wasn't home either. My father didn't know I had moved, but

Shirley was wrong to think that he would be constantly in touch. He hadn't been. And the reason, I was beginning to suspect, was that he had a new girlfriend.

I am not a suspicious person, but a few days before Shirley's departure, when I had dropped in to see Leonard at his Village apartment, I had noticed something strange. His apartment was neat. Don't get me wrong. My father is very clean and natty in his appearance, but a good housekeeper he is not. He used to drive Mom crazy with the way he dropped his clothes on the floor, and the way he would leave wet towels hanging all over the bathroom. But suddenly—suddenly—his apartment was as neat as a pin. There was even a bunch of flowers in a vase on his desk. And the inside of the refrigerator, which usually looked as though a bomb had hit a delicatessen, was organized and fresh.

The more I put the pieces together, the more I came to the conclusion that my dad was in love. He had had his steel-gray hair cut very short and was wearing a lot of new shirts. There was a new carpet in his living room. OK, I told myself, fine—because his being in love would make life easier for me. When he had been in love with Jane Anne, he had been so preoccupied he had almost forgotten my existence.

Anyway, on that first night in the barbershop, I

crawled into bed around eleven and invited the
dogs to join me. Weary from racing up and down
the room, they jumped up on the blanket. Mac-
Gregor, the Scottie, conked out at once and began
to snore—but Happy, who is part Cairn and part
Norfolk, just sat there studying me. He is a tough
little dog, with a wonderful temperament, and he
is also very smart. "Why are we here?" his expression said to me. "What's up?"

I didn't sleep well that night, because the sounds
of the city were too close. Shirley's apartment is
on the fifteenth floor of an old, solid building, and
you don't hear too much, but the barbershop was
like Grand Central Station. A fire engine screamed
by a few inches away from my bed, and then an
ambulance. "Morris," a woman's voice on the sidewalk was saying, "why can't I depend on you?"

And then there were the sounds of feet on the
pavement, and the howling of a tomcat, and a radio
blaring. "You are my lover!" sang someone over
the radio. "So don't take cover! Oh, baby, let it
rain all day."

Somehow, I fell asleep—around two A.M.—but
by six I was wide awake again because what
sounded like an army of garbage trucks had invaded
the block. Happy and MacGregor were both pressed
up against me, snoring, so I wrapped my arms

38

around them and tried to take comfort from their warm little bodies. But I'll tell you something—for a girl who had just said good-bye to everything, and was striking out on her own, I didn't feel too wonderful.

6

Before I get onto the subject of Harvey Beaumont the Third, the person who changed my life that summer, I want to tell you some more about my first days in the dog rescue business. One of the things uppermost in my mind was to be by the phone on Tuesdays and Fridays when my mother called from Europe, so there would be no snags. The first Tuesday that she called, I was standing at attention by the phone in her bedroom at ten A.M. Amazing how clear her voice sounded—as though she was around the corner.

"Paris you would not believe!" she yelled into the phone. "New buildings everywhere. It's as bad as New York. And the traffic! Bobo was almost hit by a taxi outside of our hotel. Her shoe came off."

"Are you in Paris now?" I asked, tempted to yell like she was yelling.

"No, no," she yelled, "we're in St. Tropez. We're staying with Bobo's friends the Lowenthals. A very nice couple. But the girls on the beaches here go topless, and it's really disgusting. You don't know where to look.''

"How's the weather?'' I asked, not knowing what else to say.

"The weather?'' she screamed. ''Fine. A little too hot for Bobo, but fine. She takes a siesta every afternoon. And then we all have drinks on the Lowenthals' terrace. Listen — are you all right? Tell me what you've been doing.''

"Nothing much. Just fooling around.''

"Have you been seeing your father?''

"Sure,'' I lied. ''Every day.''

"Good, good,'' she yelled. ''Listen, baby, I've got to go now because I'm using the Lowenthals' phone. It's on my charge card, but it's still their phone. We're flying to Rome tomorrow, and then Venice. I'll call you.''

"From where?'' I asked.

"Venice!'' she yelled. ''We're staying at the Gritti, which Bobo says used to be a palace.''

"Right. I'll talk to you on Friday.''

I hung up the phone with an odd realization — and this was the fact that I was now in a position to do anything I liked. With Shirley away and Leonard preoccupied, I could drink myself into a stupor, if I wanted to, or smoke grass, or have a love affair. I could go out in the middle of the night for a pizza, if I felt like it, and I could take Happy and MacGregor walking by the East River at dawn. The trouble was, I didn't want to do any of those things.

What I did instead was to place an ad for Dog Rescue, Incorporated, in *The New York Times*, order business cards from a printer, and prepare the barbershop for its future guests. I bought dog bowls and dog beds, collars and leashes, a case of dog food, and I even purchased a dog First Aid Kit at a dog boutique called Santa Paws. Then, around three days after I had settled into the barbershop, I hit the streets—looking for my first stray dogs. On this initial foray I left Happy and MacGregor at home, because I didn't know what I would find out there. Some strays can be vicious, and many are injured. In the back pocket of my jeans I had a pair of heavy leather gloves. Attached to my belt were three leashes.

Life, however, seems to be what happens while you are making other plans—because, for some reason, I could not find a single stray dog. For *three days* I roamed the Upper East Side, alert to any sign of a stray, only to find none. Before I had been in business, I had seen strays everywhere—running through the park, sitting forlornly in front of grocery stores, lying exhausted on the sidewalk in the summer heat—and now there were none. It was frustrating, if not to say maddening, because I was raring to go.

Finally, at the end of the fourth day, I came across a thin, exhausted-looking Schnauzer tied to a fire hydrant. Dogs are abandoned in this manner all the time—tied up and deserted—so very cautiously, I reached out to let him sniff me. He licked my hand in a pathetic way and gave a little woof. I untied his leash and stroked him. "It's all right, fella," I said, "don't worry. You're coming home with me."

I must say he looked grateful as I began to lead him up the block. But then I heard a shriek, and, turning around, saw that a fat woman was running after me. "Stop that girl!" she was screaming. "Stop her! She's stealing my dog!"

To make a long story short, it turned out that I had taken this woman's dog while she was shopping in the dime store. But how was I to know that? The dog *looked* like a stray—it was as thin as the woman was fat—so how was I to know the difference? At any rate, the woman was so hysterical that I couldn't reason with her. I just handed her the dog's leash and said, "I'm sorry. It was a mistake."

"*Mistake?*" she screamed. "You're lucky I'm not phoning the cops this very minute. Get the hell out of here before I have you arrested."

It was not an auspicious beginning. And so, feeling very depressed, I went back home to the barbershop, to see Happy and MacGregor and to try, for the hundredth time, to phone Chester Gilroy. I wanted to thank him for giving me the tip on the barbershop, but he was never home.

I was calling my dad every day now, so he would think that I was living at Shirley's. But true to my hunch, some major change was overtaking his life. He had joined a fitness club, he told me, and was "working out" every morning. He was thinking of buying a Honda Accord.

"But do you really need a car in the city?" I asked him. "It seems impractical."

"Not at all!" he said into the phone. "I may want to go away for some weekends this summer. Your pop has been an old stick-in-the-mud. He needs a little change."

"Where would you go?" I asked, surprised at how depressed I felt. I mean, did I *care* if he went away for a few weekends? No.

44

"I may rent a friend's house on Shelter Island. A cottage."

"But Daddy, that's such a long drive. For a week end, that is."

"We'll see, we'll see," he said happily. "But I want to know something about *you*, sweetheart. What have you been doing since your mother left?"

"Uh, I've taken a job in a bookstore. On Madison Avenue. It pays pretty well."

Leonard didn't skip a beat, which proved to me how out of touch with reality he was. Had he given my statement one second's thought, he would have realized that I am not the sort of person who works in a bookstore. "Good," he said, "good. That sounds enterprising."

"Are we having lunch this Saturday, Dad?"

"Well . . . I'm not sure. I may have to work at the office on Saturday. Let me phone you, pussy-cat."

"No, no," I said quickly. "I'll phone *you*. I'm not home much these days."

I put down the phone feeling like I had just been marooned on a desert island. The ship that had left me there was steaming away, and they had forgotten to provide me with food. Yep, there I was on an island with two small dogs and no provisions. . . . Banishing such an image, I decided to go over to Shirley's and borrow the small TV set from the den. I am very big on nature programs, and anyway, a TV would soothe this feeling that kept washing over me. A feeling very much like loneliness.

7

I met Harvey Beaumont the Third on June 26th, at three in the afternoon, and it was not exactly a monumental experience. In fact, if fate hadn't taken a hand in the whole thing, I would never have contacted him again. That's how annoying he seemed to me. How peculiar.

I was walking Happy and MacGregor in Central Park, near the 96th Street entrance, and as usual it was raining. It had been raining for most of June, a slow steady summer rain that did not make my dog-hunting activities any easier. New York was filled with strays, crowded with them, and yet with the exception of that unfortunate Schnauzer, I could not find a single one.

So there we were, Happy and MacGregor and me, trudging through the rain. Happy hated bad weather and was angry to be out in it, but MacGregor didn't mind at all. MacGregor has a sober temperament — no sense of humor — but I have always liked the way he puts up with things. Inconveniences and discomforts do not faze him. He is a Scot.

I was bending my head under the rain, which was coming down pretty hard now, when all of a sudden a dog ran past. A big dog, some kind of Setter, and definitely a stray. In the second that it streaked by me, I could see that it was skin and bones. Yep, it was an Irish Setter and it was starving.

Tying my own two dogs to a lamppost, I took off after the Irish Setter—running faster than I had ever run in my life. "Here boy, here boy!" I kept yelling. But the dog wouldn't stop. Irish Setters are very fast runners, so it began to occur to me that I wasn't going to catch him.

Suddenly I saw that someone up ahead on the path had caught him and was holding on fast. Racing up to this person, who turned out to be a small blond teenage boy, I said, "God! Thank you. I didn't think I would get him."

I stood there for a moment, trying to catch my breath, as the boy stroked the Setter and calmed him down. He was terribly small — the boy, I mean — and was dressed in faded jeans and a T-shirt. There was a preppy air about him that I recognized at once. I mean, you can't go to private school in New York and not recognize this quality. I decided that he was around fifteen years old.

"Thanks so much," I said, when I had caught my breath. "I appreciate it."

The boy gave me a shy look. I noticed that he had a camera around his neck on a wide black strap. It was protected by a plastic case. "You're entirely welcome," he said.

"I'm in the dog rescue business," I explained.

"Setters are difficult," he said, stroking the dog. "I mean, they're gun dogs that have been bred for show. So temperamentally, they're a little unsound."

"No kidding."

"They run away all the time."

"You're an expert on Irish Setters?" I asked.

He shook his head. "Not at all. But this dog is show quality—so perhaps you can find his owner. I would suggest looking in *The New York Times*. Under Lost and Found."

He was like a little old man, fussy and precise. And the more I studied him, the more I realized that he looked like Truman Capote. He probably went to some fancy school like Lawrence or Hastings. All boys.

"Well . . ." I said, taking the Setter by his worn leather collar. "Thanks a lot."

"One more thing," said the kid. "This dog looks starved, so don't overfeed him when you get home. Some kibble and water the first day would be fine."

The whole situation was beginning to annoy me. I mean, I *knew* he was trying to be helpful, but he was just so damn pompous. "Thanks for the advice," I said ironically. "You'd make a great vet."

"I probably would," he replied, "but actually, I'm a photographer. I'll give you my card."

He took a card from the back pocket of his jeans and handed it to me. On the card was engraved, "Harvey Beaumont the Third. Photography. (212) 555–2211."

I stood there staring at his card and wondering why a fifteen-year-old would have a business card in the first place. "You look a little young to be in business," I said.

"I'm eighteen. And you are . . ."

"Uh, Heidi Rosenbloom. Of Dog Rescue, Incorporated."

I handed him *my* card and he read it carefully. "Are you really incorporated?" he asked.

"Yes," I lied.

"How long have you been in business?"

"Oh, for ages," I said casually. "Our motto is 'If you lose a dog, we will find him. If you wish to adopt a dog, we will provide one.' We will also be doing grooming and boarding. Eventually."

"Interesting," said the boy, who by now I was calling Truman in my mind. "But not profitable."

Trying to keep the lid on my temper, I gave him a tolerant smile. "Is your photography profitable?"

"Not yet. But I'm not in it for profit. I'm in it to achieve something beautiful."

Well, that one had me stumped—but only momentarily. "Look," I said, "it's been nice meeting you, but I want to get this dog home. My own two dogs are over there, tied to a lamppost."

I started to stroll down the path, and so did Harvey Beaumont. Obviously, he was not going to be easy to get rid of. By now the rain had stopped and the skies over the Park were brightening. When they saw us approaching, Happy and MacGregor began to bark with joy.

"These are yours?" said Harvey Beaumont. "Nice."

"Thank you."

"The Norfolk-Cairn mix is cute, but the Scottie is first-rate. A perfect conformation."

"Harvey," I said, "you've missed your calling. You shouldn't be a photographer. You should be working for the American Kennel Club."

To my satisfaction, he blushed.

Happy and MacGregor were sniffing the Setter like mad, trying to find out who he was and where he had come from. "I have to get this dog home," I said again.

"Just one thing . . . his coat is matted now, but after you groom him, look for a tattoo somewhere on his flanks. Many dogs are tattooed these days, to help identify them if they're stolen."

"Harvey," I said, "you are an absolute *fund* of information. Good-bye."

I had put one of my spare leashes on the Setter, and he was pulling like mad. Happy and Mac-Gregor, whose leashes I held with my left hand, were pulling too. *"Au revoir,"* I said. "And thanks."

"One more thing," said Harvey, running after me. "Setters can be destructive. If you need help with him, just give me a call."

"Right," I said grimly. "Good-bye."

"I live on 82nd Street!" he called. "Just a few blocks from you."

"Farewell!" I screamed. And then I beat a hasty retreat out of the Park. As I headed homeward, to the barbershop, the Setter looked up at me with a glance that I can only call grateful. He really did know that I had rescued him, and that he was about to receive help. "You're a good boy," I said to him, as we crossed Madison Avenue. "A brave, good boy. I'll call you Brian."

8

Irish Setters, said my dog encyclopedia, are field dogs who have, unwisely, been bred for show. They are at their best not in the show ring, but out of doors where they can fulfill their purpose of "setting" the game. They need to run for miles each day and do not make satisfactory pets.

That, I decided, was putting it mildly—because Brian was turning out to be a maniac. I had taken him down to the Animal Medical Center, for an examination and shots, and while his health was OK, his temperament was not. What had I gotten into? Brian was more like a bull in a china shop than a Setter in a barbershop. He was wrecking everything I owned.

Back and forth he would race, with Happy and MacGregor at his heels. Back and forth, the length of the shop, knocking everything over as he went. He broke both my lamps and a number of coffee cups. Nervous in his new home, he peed on the floor.

Happy and MacGregor did not know what to make of him. In one way, they liked him because he played so vigorously. But in another way, he offended them. Both of my dogs have very good manners, but Brian was psychotic. It wasn't that we didn't *like* him, it was just that we couldn't control him. And also, he barked.

On his second day at the barbershop, Brian barked for two hours in a row. I tried walking him around the block several times, and I tried bribing him with dog biscuits, but he would not stop barking. Even Happy and MacGregor were growing weary of this. And then, Mr. Morganthau knocked at my door. Morganthau—the only other tenant in the building.

I opened the door a crack and looked out. "Yes?" I said.

"My name is Morganthau," he said stiffly, "and there is a tremendous amount of barking coming from this apartment. This shop, I mean. I've been trying to take a nap upstairs. It's terrible."

I looked at Mr. Morganthau and saw that he was a sallow person in his forties, dressed in an old business suit. There was a ferret in his jacket. Its little head was peeping out.

"Is that a ferret?" I said to Mr. Morganthau. "I've never seen one before."

"This is Stanley," said Mr. Morganthau. "And *he's* been trying to nap too. But we simply cannot sleep with all that barking going on. What on earth have you got in there?"

He was peering past me, trying to see what I had inside the barbershop. Stanley the ferret was peering too. He had a long thin body and a very tiny face—like a weasel's.

"I'm sorry," I said. "I've got a new dog and he hasn't adjusted to this place yet. I'm sure he won't bark forever."

"Well, if he doesn't stop barking, I am going to call the police. What are you doing here, operating a kennel?"

I thought it was a bit nervy of Mr. Morganthau to criticize my dogs, in view of the fact that he had a ferret. But ferrets, obviously, did not make noise. "Please be patient," I said. "The new dog will adjust. I promise you."

Five minutes later, Brian began to bark again. And then he began to race wildly up and down the room. Disgusted with the whole business, Happy and MacGregor sat on my bed, watching him. Back and forth, ran Brian, back and forth. But when—suddenly—he tried to hurl himself through the front windows of the shop, I knew I had had enough. *"Stop it!"* I yelled at him. *"Stop!"*

55

I put a long leash on Brian and tied him to an iron pipe that went up one wall of the barbershop. Then I sat down at my desk and studied Harvey Beaumont's business card. After a minute, I placed my own business card and that of Chester Gilroy alongside, to compare the three. My own was very cheaply printed, and Chester Gilroy's was not much better. But Harvey Beaumont the Third's was engraved. When you ran your thumb over the letters, you could feel them. And the card itself was printed on thick, cream-colored stock.

The engraved card made me think of my mother, and then I started thinking about our last phone conversation. Shirley had called me from Venice the day after she arrived, but as soon as I heard her voice I knew that something had happened.

"What's wrong?" I yelled into the phone. "Has anything happened?"

"You bet your life something has happened!" she yelled back. "Bobo fell in the Canal."

"What?"

"Heidi, stop screaming at me. This connection is perfectly good. I said—Bobo fell in the Canal. She's under a doctor's care this very moment."

Stifling my laughter, I said, "How did that happen?"

"We were taking our first gondola ride, and she stood up in the gondola to look at something. And

56

then, before you know it, she's overboard. Heidi, are you laughing?"

"No, no," I said, recovering myself. "Is she all right now?"

"I *told* you, she's under a doctor's care. It took four gondoliers to get her out of the water. And the Canal is filthy! God knows what disease she could have caught."

"Well, I'm sorry to hear all that. Otherwise, how do you like Venice?"

"Overrated would be putting it mildly. Rome and Florence I saw years ago, with your father, but Venice, no. So I thought it was going to be something special. But there's nothing to look at here but art. Religious art."

"How's the hotel? The Gritti?"

"Bobo thinks we should have stayed at the Cipriani, but it's too late to change now. The dirt in this city! Stray cats, garbage in the Canal . . . I can't wait till we get to Switzerland. Bobo says that in Zurich you could eat off the streets."

Brian's barking brought me back to the present. He was barking as though his vocal chords would snap, and all I could think of was Mr. Morganthau and Stanley, trying to get some sleep upstairs. "Quiet!" I shouted at Brian—and then I went over to the phone and dialed Harvey Beaumont's number. To hell with the fact that he was a small, annoying person who resembled Truman Capote. I needed assistance.

He picked up the phone at once. "Beaumont Photography," he said. "Beaumont speaking."

"Harvey? This is the person you met in the Park the other day. Heidi Rosenbloom. Do you remember me?"

There was a pause, and then he said, "Of course."

"Well listen, Harvey, you were right about the Setter. He *is* a little destructive. And I can't get him to stop barking."

"Did you find a tattoo on him?"

"No. I had the vet look for one, when he had his checkup, but there was nothing."

"What about ads? Have you placed any?"

"Yes. In *The Times* and *The Village Voice*."

"Hmmm," said Harvey Beaumont. "Tell me one more thing. Is he trained?"

"Harvey, I don't know. I've tried to give him obedience commands, but he acts like he doesn't hear them. He's a maniac. I'm really having trouble."

"Very well," said Harvey Beaumont in his fussy voice. "I'll come over and give you a hand. Your address is the one on your business card?"

"Yes."

"I'm only a few blocks away. I'll be there soon."

9

Harvey Beaumont arrived within a half hour—and he had a choke collar and a book on dog obedience with him. He looked just like he had looked the other day—those faded jeans, that old T-shirt—but if anything, he looked smaller. It was hard to believe that he was eighteen, and I wondered if he had lied about it.

He didn't make any comments on my living quarters. He just glanced around the place for a moment, to get the lay of the land, and then he went over to the Setter. "What do you call him?"

"Brian," I said. "It's as good a name as any."

Brian had jumped up on Harvey and was now the taller of the two. But then, I reasoned, almost anyone would be taller than Harvey Beaumont. "Brian," said Harvey, giving the hand signal for *sit*, "that's enough. *Sit!*"

To my amazement, Brian sat down.

"Sit and *stay*," said Harvey, backing away from Brian slowly. "Stay."

Brian stayed.

Harvey was standing about ten feet away from Brian. Finally, he said, "All right, Brian. *Come.*"

Quickly, Brian trotted over to Harvey. *"Sit,"* said Harvey, and once again Brian sat down.

"Wow," I said. "That's fantastic."

"What we have learned in these five minutes," said Harvey, "is that your Setter is obedience trained. He's a very good dog, really, you just didn't know the right signals." He handed me a paperback book. "I've brought you a book by Barbara Woodhouse. It explains everything."

"How did you learn all that?"

"My mother raises Setters. In our apartment."

I thought about this for a moment. "In a New York apartment, you mean?"

"Right. It makes life difficult."

I'll bet it does, I thought. Aloud, I said, "Would you like a cup of coffee, Harvey? Or a Coke or something?"

"Do you have any tea?"

How typical, I thought, that Harvey Beaumont should drink tea. "Sure," I said. "I've got some Lipton's. You want it hot, or iced?"

"Hot. With lemon, if you've got some."

He sat down on my piano bench as I went back to the kitchen and put the kettle on. "The thing you've got to remember about dogs," he called to

60

me, "is that they're pack animals. Right now, *you* are the leader of the pack, so don't be afraid of Brian. You are definitely the boss."

In a few minutes I brought him his tea, with lemon, and sat down on the wooden chair facing him.

Harvey was looking around the room. "How did you find this place? It's very interesting."

"I got a tip from a man named Chester Gilroy. A perfect stranger."

"Do you mind if I ask what rent you are paying?"

"Three fifty a month."

"Fantastic."

Since Harvey had another camera around his neck, a small one this time, I said, "What kinds of things do you photograph?"

"Vegetables," he replied. "Flowers. And sometimes, fruits."

"I beg your pardon?"

"Actually, I do all kinds of photography. But in the past few months I've gotten very involved with macro. You know—closeup work. Vegetables and fruits done this way look almost like abstract paintings. And rosebuds! I can't tell you how terrific rosebuds look up close. It's fascinating."

"Do you sell your pictures?"

His face reddened. "Not yet. I mean, I'm just starting out."

He took a sip of his tea, and I just sat there,

thinking how eccentric he was for a teenager. "Where do you go to school?" I asked.

"I just graduated. From Lawrence."

"No kidding. *I* just graduated from Spencer."

"Did you like Spencer?"

"No. I hated it."

Harvey stared at the floor. "I hated Lawrence so much that I considered committing suicide. Many times."

It was clear that he meant it. I mean, some people talk about suicide casually, almost conversationally—but I knew that this kid was sincere. "Well," I said, "I'm glad you didn't."

"They were the worst years of my life. The four years at Lawrence."

"Were you doing drugs or something?"

"No. Of course not."

"Are you going to college?"

He shook his head. "Mother made me apply to Harvard, and I actually was accepted there. But I turned them down."

"God. She must have been furious."

"That," said Harvey Beaumont, "is putting it mildly."

"What about your dad?"

Harvey finished his tea and put the empty cup on the floor. "My dad lives in Connecticut. They're separated."

62

"And what did he think?"

"He just said that he didn't mind because, after all, the best university is life."

"Wow. He sounds unusual."

"He is. He's much older than Mother. In his sixties, actually."

"I'm not going to college, either. My parents had a fit."

Harvey gave me a curious look. "Where were you supposed to go?"

"Radcliffe, but I refused to apply. I wanted to go into business instead. The dog rescue business."

Harvey rose to his feet and walked over to the bed, where Happy and MacGregor were sleeping. Gently, he stroked MacGregor. "I admire that," he said.

"Admire what?"

"Someone striking out on his own. I'd *love* to have my own apartment, but I'm just not solvent yet."

I had a sudden image of Harvey and his mother living in some dingy apartment with a lot of dogs. I could even see the small rooms and shabby furniture.

He glanced at his watch. "I've enjoyed this so much, Heidi, but I've got to scoot downtown. I have my developing done on Broome Street, where it's cheaper."

"You don't do your own developing?" I asked, walking him to the door.

"It requires too much equipment."

I was sorry that he was leaving. God knows, he was unusual—peculiar, even—but there was something nice about him all the same. "I hope you'll come again," I said. "I mean, to see how Brian is doing. I'll start working with that book you loaned me right away."

"Oh, the book isn't a loan. It's a gift."

"Well thanks, Harvey. I appreciate it."

He put out his hand and I shook it. "Thank you for the tea."

"Harvey . . . could I ask you something personal?"

He looked me straight in the eye. "Of course."

"Did you really consider suicide? Just because of school?"

"Yes, I did. Many times. But someone saved me."

"A friend, you mean?"

A sad look crossed his face. "Yes, a friend. She was twenty."

"Oh. Someone older."

"She was twenty and I was fourteen. I lived because of her."

After giving me one of his sad little smiles, he was gone—and I was left standing there, feeling more curious than I had felt about anyone for a long time. I knew he was fussy and odd—and he was shorter than I was, which, believe me, is *short*—but Harvey Beaumont had just revealed to me that he had a past.

10

Harvey didn't phone me again, and I found that very strange. We had had a certain rapport that day in the barbershop—I had even thought he was attracted to me—but the phone did not ring. To hell with it, I told myself, you are better off alone. Just look back over your life, Heidi, and see what a mess you have made of relationships. Go it alone, Heidi. Be brave.

Meanwhile, I was not only having success in training Brian, but had acquired another dog. Reaching Chester Gilroy by phone one night, to thank him for the tip on the barbershop, he had revealed that his friend on Horatio Street could no longer keep her Chihuahua. She was an executive who traveled, and her schedule was tight. "Would you take him?" Chester asked. "I mean, you've just told me that you're in the dog rescue business."

I didn't want to tell Chester that the only dog in the world I am not in love with is the Chihuahua, because his voice was slightly suspicious—as though he didn't believe that I was really in business. On the other hand, *was* I in business? So far, I had spent three thousand dollars of my savings and not earned one cent. "Would she like to board him with me?" I asked. "We will also be doing boarding and grooming. Eventually."

"No, no, she needs to get rid of him. She'll reimburse you, of course, for his expenses."

"How old is he?"

"Ten. His name is Pablo."

I tried to imagine myself finding a home for an elderly Chihuahua named Pablo, and failed. "Well . . ."

"You know," said Chester, "I *did* give you the tip on that barbershop. And you're paying a terribly low rent. I myself had to take a sublet on East 24th. One thousand a month."

"OK, Chester," I said. "OK. When do you want me to take him?"

"We'll bring him over tonight. In a cab."

That evening, Chester and his friend Tracy arrived at my door with a small, mean, elderly Chihuahua. Thrusting twenty bucks into my hand, for dog food, they made conversation for a few minutes and then they split. So now, in addition to Happy and MacGregor and Brian, I was the owner of a Chihuahua.

After investigating him, Happy and MacGregor stayed clear of Pablo, but Brian took a lively interest. He thought he was a puppy or something, and started acting paternal. But walking the four of them was almost impossible because Pablo could not keep up with the rest. I had to walk him separately, and thus had to endure the comments of passersby. One cab driver even shouted at me, "Hey girlie. What's on the end of that leash? A mouse?"

Mother and Bobo were due home on July 3rd, and I had decided to meet them at Kennedy Airport. However, since life is definitely the thing that happens while you are making other plans, it didn't turn out that way. Because one afternoon, while I was back at Shirley's apartment borrowing some food from the freezer, I received an emergency call from her. "Heidi!" she screamed into the phone. "Can you hear me? This connection is awful."

"Yes, yes, I can hear you," I replied. "How come you're calling at this hour?"

"We were robbed!" she screamed. "Yesterday, in broad daylight. Two men ran off with our purses! And in these purses was everything we own. Plane tickets, travelers' checks, passports, everything."

"Mom," I said, "please calm down. Tell me where you are."

"Zurich! And this is the one place we were assured that nobody robs you. Right in the middle of the day we were robbed, in a shopping mall underneath the railway station. Bobo ran after them, but they got away.''

''What are you going to do?''

''We've already been to the American Embassy and they tell us they will handle the whole thing. But we'll be delayed coming home.''

''God, I'm so sorry,'' I said. ''Is there anything I can do?''

''No, no,'' she screamed, ''but you can imagine what a wreck Bobo is. The only nice thing is that we're staying at a good hotel, the Baur au Lac. And if this hadn't happened, we would have *loved* Switzerland. You could eat off the streets here, and the shops are fabulous.''

''Do you want me to tell Daddy what happened?''

''No,'' she said, ''Or maybe yes. I don't know. Tell him if you want to. Are you all right, baby? Is everything OK?''

''Sure. I'm fine. But the weather is awful. In the nineties.''

''Baby, I have to go now. But I'll phone you before we come back.''

''No, no,'' I said quickly, ''let me phone *you*. I have a summer job in a bookstore. I'm not home very much.''

Shirley gave me the number of the Baur au Lac, and then she hung up, leaving me with the image of Bobo Lewis—all three hundred pounds of her—chasing two robbers through a shopping mall.

By the first of July, I had placed five ads for Pablo the Chihuahua in various newspapers and magazines. Describing him as a bright, cheerful little dog who would make anyone a good pet, I sat by the phone and waited. But no one in the entire city of New York, obviously, wanted to adopt a Chihuahua. I had also done a flier on both Brian and Pablo, and spent part of each day sticking these fliers into mailboxes in vestibules. Last but not least, I was taping homemade signs about Dog Rescue, Incorporated, on utility poles.

One humid night I woke up from a bad dream and wished that I had someone to talk to. I had only been living alone for a few weeks, but God, how lonely I was. I needed a friend, a confidante, someone I could share things with. Someone to turn to when things got bad.

I switched on the lights and went to the kitchen for a Coke. Happy and MacGregor were each sleeping in a barber chair, and Pablo was sleeping in Brian's arms, on the floor. Brian's character had been improving rapidly, and now he had this thing about Pablo.

It was one A.M., and somewhere in the neighborhood a person was playing the piano. I got myself
a Coke, turned off the lights and went back to bed —
wondering why Harvey Beaumont the Third had
dropped me. He had seemed so eager to know
me that first day in the Park, and he had also been
eager to come over to the shop. And then . . .
nothing.

I lay there in the darkness, sipping the Coke
and listening to that piano music — classical — and
then, like a silent film, my love life began to pass
before my eyes. Not that I had *had* much of a love
life. But a couple of years ago I had fallen in love
with a boy named Jeffrey — a dancer who was trying
to break into show business — and the whole thing
had been very painful because Jeffrey was gay. Like
Harvey Beaumont's friend, Jeffrey had been twenty
years old, and though we had become friends, he
had never reciprocated my feelings. . . . After that,
I had had a weird experience with my English
teacher Mr. Moss, who had developed a crush on
me, and that was all. Neither of those experiences
had lasted very long, and both had been chaste.
Oh, Lionel Moss and I had kissed a lot — he had
quit his job at Spencer lest the whole thing worry
his conscience — but it never went further than that,
and eventually he had gone back to live with his

aunt in Virginia. It was this experience that had persuaded me to give up men, because it showed me that my judgment stank.

On the other hand, I was beginning to feel that I was the last teenage virgin in New York—because everyone I knew was making out with someone. Even my friend Veronica in L.A., who is a rather cautious person, had finally gone to bed with a boy named C.C. whose passion was old automobiles, and true to the bargain we'd made, she had sent me a telegram the morning after. "It happened," said the telegram. "Boring. Love, Veronica."

I finished the last of my Coke and went back to the kitchen, where the phone was. Was Harvey Beaumont the Third the kind of person who would be awake at one thirty A.M.? Yes, I told myself, he was.

He picked up the phone at once. "Beaumont Photography," he said. "Beaumont speaking."

"Harvey? It's me. Heidi Rosenbloom."

I heard him catch his breath, and then there was silence. "Are you there?" I asked.

"Yes. I am."

"Is it OK for me to call you at this hour? Were you asleep?"

"Oh no, not at all. I was just studying some transparencies."

"Transparencies?"

"Slides. Of vegetables."

"Oh, right. Listen—I just wanted to tell you that Brian is doing very well. He's calmed down and everything. But I still haven't found him a home."

"Did you advertise?"

"Of course. But it's costing a fortune."

"I know. Everything does."

"I've acquired another dog, too. A Chihuahua."

"Oh, my. Do you like Chihuahuas?"

"No, I hate them. And this one is ten years old. Very nervous and yappy. Brian's adopted him, though, which is sort of nice."

There was a pause, and so to fill it, I said, "How are you, Harvey? How's the photography?"

"Fine," he said. "You know, I've been wanting to call you for days."

For some reason, my heart skipped a beat. "No kidding. Why didn't you?"

"I . . . I wasn't quite sure that you liked me. I didn't want to impose."

"*Like* you? Of course I like you. Why would I phone you if I didn't like you?"

"I just wasn't sure, that's all. I mean, you seem so busy and everything. With your dog rescue business. So successful."

I laughed. "Harvey, old pal, I have spent three

thousand dollars on this business in three weeks —
but have yet to earn a penny. If things keep going
this way, I'll have to move back home."

"Ah. I see."

"In fact, Harvey, what I am turning out to be is
a nonprofit organization. And my dad did not raise
his daughter to be nonprofit."

"What does he do? Your dad, I mean."

"He has a jewelry business on West 47th Street."

"Heidi," said Harvey Beaumont. "Would you
like me to come over? We could talk."

"At two in the morning?"

"Sure. Why not?"

"What would your mother think?"

"She never knows what I do. She's involved with
her own life."

"Well . . . OK. Come on over. Bring some potato
chips, or peanuts or something. I have a longing
for something salty."

"Right," said Harvey, "right." He sounded very
excited. "Is there anything else I can bring you?
Something for the dogs?"

"No, no, just some peanuts or potato chips."

"A carton of milk? Some dog food?"

"All I want is *peanuts*, Harvey. Planters."

11

Harvey Beaumont arrived at two thirty A.M. with a can of Planters peanuts, a package of Charles potato chips, a pound of Italian salami and a packet of cream cheese. He had also brought with him two large bottles of Coke and a small selection of pastries. "Where did you get all that food?" I asked him. "It's the middle of the night."

He grinned at me. "This is New York."

He had dressed up in a clean pair of jeans and a blue shirt with a button-down collar. I, on the other hand, was still in my boy's cotton bathrobe and old slippers.

We took the food back to the kitchen and spread it out on the table. Surprised at being wakened in the middle of the night, all four dogs padded into the kitchen and sat down. Brian was eyeing the salami.

"I'll make us salami-and-cream-cheese sandwiches," I said to Harvey. "God, those pastries look good. Did you find an all-night bakery?"

"No, they're from our pantry. My mother had guests for dinner."

For a while we ate in silence, refusing to give handouts to the dogs, who were whimpering like they hadn't been fed for a year. "Do you always stay up late?" I asked Harvey, as I chewed my sandwich.

"Yes," he said. "It's a good time to look at slides. The apartment is so quiet."

"Do you study, Harvey? Photography, I mean."

He blushed. "Not yet. I'm teaching myself at the moment."

You certainly blush easily, I thought. Aloud, I said, "I guess you always wanted to be a photographer. Right?"

He seemed surprised. "Oh no, not at all. For a long time, I wanted to be a writer—and I even got a story published once, in a magazine—but all I ever wrote were horror stories and it seemed a bit limiting."

I pondered this for a moment. "In what way?"

He took a sip of Coke and patted his lips with a napkin. "Well, in the sense that I couldn't seem to write in any other form. You know?"

"Not really."

He gave me his shy smile. "It's this way. Literature is based on *forms*. The poem, the short story, the

76

novel, etc. But I couldn't seem to learn any of them. The only thing I was able to do was write horror stories, stories in which terrible things happened to people. Gruesome stories with unhappy endings."

"Give me an example."

"Well . . . I once wrote a story in which a boy locks his sister in an enormous scooped-out pumpkin and just keeps her there, year after year. Eventually, she goes mad."

"Wow."

"And my father felt that it was all a bit limiting. I mean, he's really a very encouraging person, but he felt the whole thing was too narrow."

"So you went into photography."

"Right. I decided that I might be better with images than words, so I went out and bought a camera and started to experiment. I'm not too bad, either, if I do say so myself."

He took a bite of sandwich and sat there staring at the floor, and once again I was struck by his resemblance to Truman Capote. Shirley has an old book in her bookcase called *Other Voices, Other Rooms*, by Capote, and on the back cover is a picture of the author as a very young man. Round face, blond bangs, serious eyes. And this picture looked just like Harvey.

"Has anyone ever told you that you resemble Truman Capote?" I asked.

Once again, Harvey blushed. "Yes."

"He's dead now, I think."

"It's true," said Harvey, "he is. As they said in the papers, 'He died of everything.'"

Harvey Beaumont, I said silently, you are just too weird for words. On the one hand, you have no confidence at all—and yet on the other, you talk like an elderly stockbroker. You are a strange mixture of shyness and *chutzpah* and I do not understand you.

He was stroking MacGregor, who sat at his feet looking at him in a worshipful way. When you thought about it, the two of them were alike. Charming, but no sense of humor. Born old.

"Harvey . . . would you be willing to tell me about your friend? The one who kept you from committing suicide."

He looked startled. "Would you be interested?"

I leaned forward, across the kitchen table, and said, "Yes."

He rose to his feet and began to walk around the tiny kitchen. He seemed nervous. "It's this way," he said. "When I was fourteen I met a girl named Chandler Brown on the Fifth Avenue bus, and I fell in love with her. I even lived with her, in a way. I mean, I slept at her place at night, and then went home every morning to get ready for school. My mother didn't notice."

"Wow," I said. It was all I could think of saying.

Harvey was pacing back and forth. "She was an actress — an aspiring actress from Grosse Pointe, Michigan, and she was very beautiful. I mean, she was so beautiful that I sometimes had trouble looking at her. Her beauty hurt me."

"I understand," I said quietly.

"Eventually, she went back to Grosse Pointe, because she had a little daughter there and she wanted to raise her. She just gave up the theater and went back to Grosse Pointe."

"Did she ever write you?"

"No. I never heard from her again."

For some reason, I wanted to go over and pat his shoulder — but I didn't. "I was in love with someone older, too. His name was Jeffrey."

Harvey sat down at the kitchen table. "Really?"

"Yes, and he was twenty too. Isn't that odd? And *also*, he was in the theater. Just like your friend."

"What a strange coincidence!"

"Isn't it? I fell for him much too hard. It was stupid of me."

Harvey leaned towards me across the table. "Why was it stupid?"

"Because he was gay."

"Ah, I see."

To my amazement, there was a lump in my throat. "Being me—stupid me—I thought I could change him. Make him go straight and everything. But of course it didn't work."

"No," said Harvey Beaumont. "Of course not."

"He went to California with some friends and I never saw him again. And he didn't write. Not even a postcard."

Harvey reached out and took my hand. "I'm sorry."

"It's OK. Really."

"We were both too needy," he said.

"Huh?"

"You and I. Obviously, we were both too needy. And that's why neither of those relationships worked out. A person can't be *needy*, Heidi, because it turns other people off."

"I guess you're right. I never thought of it that way."

The fact that he was holding my hand distressed me. I was absolutely positive that I didn't want to be involved with anyone right now—and if I *had* wanted to be involved, it wouldn't be with Harvey Beaumont. Someone who looked like a child and talked like an elderly stockbroker. I took my hand away.

"I haven't been involved with anyone since Chandler," Harvey said. "I haven't wanted to."

"How many years has it been?"

"Four."

I gazed at him. "Harvey, four years is a long time. Haven't you dated anyone since then?"

"No."

"Or been attracted to anyone?"

He glanced at me, and then he glanced away. "No. Not until now."

Well, that one threw me. So I rose to my feet and began to pace the kitchen. "Uh, Harvey, I'm not really available right now. For a relationship, I mean. I've made too many mistakes with men in the past few years and I don't think I'm ready."

"Then let's be friends," he said quickly. "Would that be all right? For us to be friends?"

I smiled. "Friendship would be fine. I could use a friend."

"Me too. I'm a very solitary person."

"We could do things together. You know, go places."

"And I could help you with the dogs. I'm really quite good with dogs."

81

"It's true," I said. "You are."

He held out his right hand. "It's a deal then? Friendship?"

"You've got it," I replied, as I shook his hand. "Friendship all the way."

12

Mother and Bobo returned from Europe on July 7th, and Bobo's butler and I met them at the airport. I did not expect them to be in high spirits, but neither did I expect them to be so depressed. Each of them had two shopping bags full of souvenirs, and their clothes were rumpled from the flight, and Bobo had had a few martinis—which do not sit well with her. On the drive back to Manhattan, we were all very quiet.

Bobo dropped us off at the apartment, and as soon as we were upstairs, Shirley took off her shoes and collapsed on the living-room couch. I was busy dragging in her suitcases from the hall. "I'm a wreck," she said, "a total wreck. I mean, Bobo is a wonderful person and all that, but as a traveling companion she is very difficult."

"Did you have any fun at all?" I asked.

Shirley sighed. She was wearing a summer pants suit, and three strands of pearls. Her makeup was a little smeared and she looked exhausted. "Fun? Fun, I don't know about. Too many terrible things happened to us."

"How was London? Did you see any plays?"

She grunted. "The only thing I saw in London was traffic." She sat up on the couch and ran one hand through her hair. "I'll tell you one thing, baby, you never appreciate this country until you leave it. This is the best country in the world, only none of us realize it. Some of the people in Europe don't even have indoor toilets."

"No kidding," I said. But privately, I was wondering what was going to happen when Shirley passed my room, on the way to her own, and saw that it was empty. What would happen when she saw that I had taken the television set from the den and all the blue sheets from the linen closet? What would she say when she realized that I had moved?

She was rummaging around in the shopping bags, looking for the presents she had brought me. And as I watched her, my heart sank—because Shirley's presents are never appropriate. She loves to give me things like shortie nightgowns and traveling makeup kits, whereas I would much rather have something practical. A Swiss army knife. A compass.

"Here are your presents," she said, "and I hope

you like them, baby, because Bobo and I spent a lot of time shopping for you. We thought of you every minute."

I looked at the things she had spread out on the coffee table. A lace see-through blouse from Venice, a cowbell from Zurich. From Paris, some Chanel No. 5. From London, a pair of "mod" pink enamel earrings. In addition to which, there were six embroidered handkerchiefs. From Belgium.

"Gee," I said. "Thanks."

"I know you think handkerchiefs are old-fashioned, but someday you'll be glad to own these. They're handmade. And Bobo and I thought the blouse would look adorable on you. Try it on, sweetie, let's see how you look. And the earrings, too."

I took off my boy's shirt and put on the see-through blouse. Then I put on the earrings and went over to the mirror by the love seat and stared at myself. I looked like a female impersonator.

"Cute," said Shirley with satisfaction. "Very very cute. . . . God, I'm so tired from that flight. What I need is a shower and a nap."

She rose to her feet and headed for her room. Tense as a board, I waited for the explosion to come—as she passed *my* room—but there was none. The next thing I heard was her shower running. She hadn't noticed my empty bedroom.

Shirley took a warm shower, lay down on her bed, and was asleep instantly. Not knowing what to do with myself, I wandered around the apartment, feeling more and more peculiar.

I sat down on the living-room couch and thought about Harvey Beaumont. In the past few days we had walked my dogs in the Park together, had dinner a few times at The Giraffe, a place on Second Avenue, and gone to a photography show at the Museum of Modern Art. We had given Pablo a bath in my kitchen sink and bought him a tiny dog bed, because he didn't like the one I had provided him. We had composed ads for Brian and placed them in various newspapers. "Offered for adoption:" said one of these ads. "Young, well-bred Irish Setter. Male. Marvelous temperament. Great with children." Nobody had responded. If things continued this way, I would not only be a nonprofit organization, but a bankrupt one. The way I was spending money was unreal. Newspaper ads, business stationery, dog food. Cabs, to go back and forth to the vet. A grooming bill, for Happy and MacGregor, of one hundred dollars. Unfortunately, Pablo was the only one of my dogs small enough to be bathed in the kitchen sink. The rest of them I took to Canine Magic, over on the West Side.

Harvey had been reluctant to invite me to his

apartment, but finally, shyly, he had asked me to come this evening—for "coffee and dessert," as he put it. The address he had written down for me was a bit startling—a building on Fifth Avenue and 82nd—but I still thought of him as poor. His clothes were so shabby. And he had told me that he cut his own hair, to save money. And then there was his film developing, which he did in Lower Manhattan, because it was cheaper, and his dismay at my casual use of cabs. Yes, I told myself, despite his Fifth Avenue address, it was obvious that he was poor. He had probably gone through Lawrence on a scholarship.

I turned on the television set near the couch, and was just about to settle down and watch an old movie, when there was a shriek from my bedroom. A shriek—and then a wail. "Heidi!" my mother screamed. "Come in here! Quickly!"

Here it comes, I told myself. Stay calm. The whole point is to stay calm.

I hurried into my bedroom and found Shirley standing in the middle of the empty room with one hand pressed to her forehead. "We've been robbed!" she said. "Someone has been in here and taken all the furniture."

"Mom . . ."

"Heidi," she said, "I want you to call the police

and tell them that we've been robbed. How could they have taken all your things? Even that junk you collect off the streets is gone. And your books are gone too! Everything you own!"

"Mother . . ."

"Who would do such a thing? Your bed, your bureau, your desk . . ." She opened my closet door. "And your clothes too! It must have happened while we were at the airport."

"Mother . . ."

"We have to call the police."

I took her by the arm. "Mother, we have *not* been robbed. It's just that I've moved out. That's all."

She stared at me. "What?"

"I moved out. While you were in Europe."

She looked at me in disbelief. "What are you saying?"

"I moved. To a place on 81st Street. It's very nice, really. You'll have to come over and see it."

Shirley sank down on the one chair I had left in the room, a little velvet boudoir chair. "This is some kind of a joke?"

I knelt by her side. "No, Mom, it isn't. I've moved away. It was time."

"*Time?* Do you know how old you are?"

"Do I know how old I am? Yes."

"You are seventeen, Heidi Rosenbloom, and people your age do not leave home. *I* didn't leave my mother's house till the day I got married."

"I'll be eighteen in September. And anyway, times are different now."

"Oh, yes? And how, may I ask, are times different? Nobody age seventeen leaves home."

"Well, I have. I've rented an empty barbershop—just for eight months. I want you to come and see it. It's nice."

"A *barbershop*?"

"And I have my own business, too. It's called Dog Rescue, Incorporated, and our motto is 'If you have lost a dog, we will find him. If you wish to adopt a dog, we will provide one.' "

"I don't believe any of this. You're making some kind of a joke."

I rose to my feet. "Sorry. I'm not."

She rose too, and stared me in the eye. "And what does your father have to say?"

"Well, he doesn't really know about it yet."

"You told me you were seeing him frequently. And you also told me you were working in a bookstore."

"Lies. I'm sorry."

"Lies? And since when are you a liar? You've always been truthful with me. Always."

"Mom," I said, "I have a right to my life."

Well, that one caught her up short, but only for a second. "Not at seventeen, you don't. What are you living on?"

"My savings."

"And how long do you think *they* will last? I'm sorry, Heidi, but you'll have to come back home. I insist on it."

"I've acquired some more dogs," I said. "A Setter and a Chihuahua. So if I come back here, they'll be coming too. That makes four dogs."

"Don't be ridiculous. You know we can't have four dogs in this apartment. We'll be evicted."

"Well, that's why I'm living in a barbershop," I said with satisfaction. "The building takes dogs. I mean, the man upstairs, Mr. Morganthau, even has a ferret."

"Heidi," said my mother, "I am going into my room to phone your father this very minute. And then we'll see what's to be done. But I can tell you one thing—*no one* in our family has ever lived in a barbershop."

13

I arrived at Harvey Beaumont's apartment house at eight that evening—and the first thing that threw me was that it was a very elegant building, with sculpture in the lobby and a doorman who had to phone your name upstairs before you could board the elevator.

The second thing that threw me was that a butler answered Harvey's door. That's right, a butler. I rang the bell, waited for a few minutes, and then this elderly butler—in uniform—opened the door. He had an English accent.

"Good evening," he said to me. "Miss Rosenbloom?"

"Uh, yes," I said.

"Master Harvey is expecting you. Right this way, please."

You could have knocked me over with a feather. Because the last thing I expected was that Harvey would be living this way. On Fifth Avenue. With a butler.

The man was leading me down a long hallway, off of which many rooms radiated. God! I thought to myself, how big *is* this place?

We passed a living room and a dining room and a library. We passed various bedrooms and baths. Finally, we arrived at a door made of paneled wood. The butler knocked on it. "Come in!" said Harvey's voice.

"Hi," he said, as the butler ushered me into the room. "I see you've met Holmes."

"Well, yes," I replied. "In a way."

"Holmes," said Harvey, "could we have our cake and coffee in about a half hour? I want to show Miss Rosenbloom around."

"Very good, Master Harvey," said the butler. And then, silently, he was gone.

"Harvey," I said, "what are you doing with a butler?"

He laughed. "Well, he's not exactly mine. He's Mother's. She's had him for years."

Before I could get a good look at Harvey's room, he led me out into the hall again, intent on showing me the apartment. Apartment? It was more like a hotel. It just went on and on.

Books, antiques, old Persian rugs. Draperies and grand pianos. Four bedrooms and four baths. Somewhere behind the pantry and kitchen, "servants' quarters." I was amazed. Because on the one hand, I had never seen such an elegant apartment—while on the other hand, its elegance was seedy. The Persian rugs all had stains on them, and some of the antique chairs had broken legs, and there was a big glass breakfront whose glass was cracked. "Mother raises Irish Setters," Harvey explained. "They take a toll on the apartment."

By way of illustrating this, he opened the door to the den, where two elderly Irish Setters were sitting on a leather couch, watching television. "These two are Thoren Oakenshield and William Arthur Muldoon," Harvey explained. "They're very old. We do have some puppies, however, in the dining room."

He led me down the hall again, into a huge room with a long dining table, a long sideboard, and a chandelier. In a box lined with newspaper three Setter puppies were sleeping. "Mother adopted them just the other day," Harvey whispered. "Let's not wake them."

Feeling more and more confused, I followed Harvey back to his room. "Your mother's a dog breeder?" I asked.

Harvey shut the door behind us and sat down on his bed. "Well yes, in a way. Her great passion in life is Setters, and she even ran an Irish Setter rescue organization for a while—sort of like you, Heidi—but her activities are limited these days because she's writing a book."

"No kidding," I said, sitting down in a leather chair. "On what?"

"It's called *The Field Dog in America*. It's her second book. A small publisher, of course."

"Of course," I said, staring at Harvey's room.

The room was almost bare. A bed and a bureau, and then just a long wooden table on which his photo equipment was arranged. Different cameras and different lenses. Cartons of Kodak film. Floodlights. And at one end of the table were groupings of vegetables and fruits. Broccoli, cauliflower, and eggplant. Cantaloupes.

"Where are your photos?" I asked. "Don't you put them on the wall?"

Harvey blushed. "My mother doesn't like them very much. I keep them in the closet."

"So take them *out* of the closet, Harvey. I'd like to see them."

His face was bright red, but he went over to the closet, pulled out a step stool and stood on it. Then he reached up to a high shelf and brought down a flat cardboard box. "Here they are. But you probably won't like them."

He opened the cardboard box and spread out

his photos on the long table. They were 8 × 12 color enlargements, and they were all closeups of vegetables. Harvey was right. They did look like abstract paintings. They were wonderful.

"These are terrific!" I said. "Really terrific. Show me some more."

Harvey took out some pictures of fruits. There was a closeup of a plum that I found quite beautiful. And many closeups of bananas. "The *compositions* are so interesting," I said.

"Aren't they?" said Harvey. "Here—let me show you what I've done with roses."

He spread out some 8 × 12 photos of roses. Some were just tightly furled buds, but others were blowsy, open roses. He had shot straight down into them, into their centers.

"God," I said, "they're so sensual. If you don't mind my saying so."

He shook his head. "Not at all. I agree with you entirely. You see, what I've tried to do here is capture the essence of these flowers. And the macro mode— or closeup—does that."

I took some more photos from him and spread them out on the table. Daisies—photographed so closely that their golden centers seemed to vibrate. Iris—velvety and purple and mysterious. "Do you ever do people?" I asked.

"Uh, no. To tell you the truth, I'm not good with people at all."

"What other kind of photos have you done?"

"I started out with insects. Dead ones, of course. Butterflies and moths. Tiger beetles. I have a whole collection of those, but I'll show them to you another time."

"It's too bad you don't put some on the wall."

"It would annoy Mother."

Holmes tapped on the door and came in with a tray on which there was a coffee service and a plate of little petit fours. "Thank you, Holmes," said Harvey. "That looks nice."

"If you require anything else, Master Harvey, please ring. I will be in my quarters."

"Right. Thank you."

As Holmes withdrew, Harvey put some petit fours on a plate and handed them to me. "Milk in your coffee?" he asked.

"Yes," I said. "Harvey?"

"Hmmm?" he said, busy with the coffee.

I forgot what I was going to say, as I regarded Harvey's torn jeans and clean, but threadbare shirt. His ragged blond bangs. His empty bedroom. Then my eye caught a small photograph in a silver frame, on top of the bureau. I went over to look at it.

The photo was the size of a snapshot, and it

showed the head and shoulders of a girl with long blond hair. She had a beautiful, but world-weary face—as though, inside, she was much older than her years—and somehow, I knew that she was Chandler Brown.

Harvey was watching me. "Yes," he said, "that's Chandler. She gave me that picture just before she went back home. To Michigan."

"She's beautiful."

A look of pain crossed Harvey's face. "I know."

I put down my coffee cup and went over to sit beside him, on the bed. "You still love her, don't you Harvey?"

He glanced away from me. "I don't know. . . . Yes, I guess I do."

"Did you have a physical relationship?"

"Oh no, it wasn't like that at all. We were just friends."

"But you wanted more?"

"Yes. Towards the end, I did."

His face was so sad that I reached out and patted his hand. "Did she . . . reciprocate your feelings?"

"Not really. She thought of me as her child. I was only fourteen, you see. And she was a very *old* twenty."

"Some people are born old, I guess."

"It's true. They are."

He took a sip of his coffee and stared at the floor. He seemed a million miles away.

"One has to go on," I said.

"Hmmm?"

I took his hand and held it between my own. "I said, Harvey, that one has to go on. I mean, it's awful for you to be hung up on someone you knew four years ago. She's probably a different person now. Just like you are."

"I still dream about her."

"Oh Harvey, do you?"

He looked at me and I saw that there were tears in his eyes. "Silly, isn't it? I dream about her all the time. And about Christina, her little girl."

"Happy dreams?"

"Oh sure, they're happy. But then I wake and realize—all over again—that she's gone."

The tears were coming down his face now, and I was impressed that he wasn't ashamed of them. I have known very few boys who will let you see them cry, but Harvey Beaumont didn't seem to mind. The tears kept on coming. Slow, silent tears.

I put my arm around his shoulder, and then I pressed my cheek against his damp cheek. "It'll be all right, Harvey, don't worry. It will all work out."

"Why do you say that?" he said in a strangled voice. "Very little in this world works out."

"That's not true."

"Yes, it is."

"You need more faith."

He turned and buried his face in my shoulder — and I just sat there, feeling partly like his mother, and partly like his friend, and . . . I don't know. There were too many feelings swimming around inside of me, and I couldn't sort them out. "I've got to be going," I said. "I have to walk the dogs."

He took out a handkerchief and blew his nose. "Must you?"

I rose to my feet and stretched. "Yes, I really must. But maybe we'll do something together tomorrow. Would you like that?"

His round little face lit up. "Yes. I would."

Harvey walked me back down the hallway. The apartment was very quiet, and I wondered where his mother was. "Is your mother home?" I asked.

"She's working on her book at a friend's apartment. Miss Kamp."

We stood together by the front door. I gazed around me for a moment, and then I laughed. "Harvey — the one thing I did *not* expect you to be was rich."

He looked baffled. "Rich? We're not rich, Heidi. Comfortable, perhaps, but not rich. In fact, my dad has just had a number of setbacks in the market, which is why I'm being so frugal these days. I don't want to take more money from him than I have to."

"Right."

"It was wonderful to have you here. I hope you'll come again."

"I will, Harvey. And thank you for the coffee and everything."

He gazed at me with the sad eyes of a Spaniel. "Heidi . . . could I kiss you good night?"

I shook my head. "No, old boy, you can't. Because it's friendship, remember? Friendship all the way."

He grinned at me. "Sorry. You're absolutely right."

14

Two days after she returned from Europe, Shirley phoned me to announce that she and my father were coming over that very evening. "This evening!" I said. "But that doesn't give me enough time!"

"For what?" she said suspiciously.

"Never mind," I said. "This evening would be great."

God! I thought, as I hung up the phone, they're going to throw the book at me. They're going to come over here, and hate it, and insist that I return home. Maybe they'll take legal action against me. I'm still a minor.

In a frenzy, I cleaned the barbershop from top to bottom, rushed out and bought new collars for the four dogs, rushed out *again* and bought some fancy pastries from a place on First Avenue—and then, once again, I rushed out. To buy flowers. To buy some Beefeater gin, in case my dad wanted a drink. To buy Shirley's favorite tea. How incredible that they were coming over together. Except for my graduation ceremony, togetherness was not exactly their thing.

"Now I want all of you to behave," I said to the dogs. "This is an important event for me, so I want you to try, try, try to behave."

As though I was inspecting the troops, I reviewed my four dogs, who were sitting in a row. Each of them had been bathed recently—Pablo in the kitchen sink, the rest at Canine Magic—and they looked pretty good. And now that I knew him better, Pablo was not really annoying. I mean, I found his smallness—small bed, small bowls, small portions of food—rather amusing, and so did Brian. Brian had developed an absolute crush on Pablo, and insisted on sleeping with him every night.

By seven thirty that evening, the barbershop looked great, the dogs looked great, and even *I* looked great—in a new pair of jeans and a Mexican blouse from the thrift shop. I had put out a tray of pastries and coffee cups, and I had bought an ashtray—in case my dad was smoking again. Then my buzzer buzzed, and I rushed to the door.

It was a shock to see them together. I mean, it suddenly took me back to the old days. As though nothing had ever happened between them—as though they were still a pair. "Hi," I said gaily. "Come in."

Gingerly, my parents stepped into the barbershop. And the minute they did, the dogs were all over them. I had not yet been able to train my four pets not to jump on people.

"Down, boys!" Leonard was saying with good humor—but my mother was walking around the place in a state of shock. "She wasn't kidding," she said to my father. "It's a barbershop."

"I told you it was a barbershop," I said, trying to keep my voice light and cheerful.

"It's a barbershop," Shirley said to my father. "Look at the chairs."

"Well, if times get tough she can always give a few haircuts," Leonard replied. He meant it as a joke, but no one laughed.

"God, Heidi," said my mother, "what a place. Do you have a kitchen? A bathroom?"

"Of course," I said, in my new, light, cheerful tone. "In the back."

My mother marched to the back room, to have a look, and my dad and I smiled at each other. He was at least ten pounds thinner, and he had a crew cut and a tan. He was wearing a pair of gray slacks and a beige shirt. "You look great," I said. "I'm glad to see you."

Except for one brief lunch date in the Village, I had not seen him for a month. And yes, I was absolutely certain now that he had a new girlfriend. His tan was so perfect. And his clothes were like something out of *Esquire*. "It's been a month," I said.

He came over and hugged me. "I know that, baby, and I feel awful about it. But your old man's been swamped at the office. And I've been going away weekends—to that house on Shelter Island I rented."

"What do you really think of this place, Daddy?"

Leonard smiled. "Well, it's a little weird, but the neighborhood is good. Which is what I said to your mother on the way over. Shirley, I said, she's in the same neighborhood you are. She's only a few blocks away."

Was this the same man who had recently burst into tears at the news that I would not be going to college? Was this the same person who had told me I had broken his heart? The same person who wanted his daughter to be Ivy League, Phi Beta Kappa, rich and successful? No, it was not—and the only explanation was love.

"The toilet has a pull chain," said Shirley, joining us again. "And she doesn't even have a stove. A hot plate, a tiny refrigerator, and a sink so small you couldn't wash a dish in it."

"Not true," I said. "I wash my Chihuahua in it all the time."

A few minutes later we were all sitting in barber chairs, having our drinks. I did have the piano bench and one wooden chair, but for some reason we wound up in the barber chairs. Shirley was having iced tea, but Leonard had chosen gin with a splash of tonic. And in my nervousness, I had put some gin into my Coke. Don't get me wrong. I rarely drink, and I have never done drugs. But their visit was unsettling.

The three of us sat there, staring into the long mirror that faced the barber chairs, and, because it was easier, we talked to one another in the mirror. "The floor of that shower is so rusty you could catch tetanus from it," said Shirley. "At least, put down a rubber mat."

"OK," I said, sipping my Coke. "I'll get one."

"And, baby, that refrigerator! It has an odor."

"Mother," I said firmly, "this is *my* place. Not yours, and not Daddy's, but mine."

"It's true," said Leonard. "It's her place. Let her do what she wants with it."

Shirley glared at my father in the mirror. "That's not what you said in the cab coming over here. In the cab, you were worried."

"The place isn't as bad as I thought. And the neighborhood is fine. You're both in the same neighborhood, for God's sake. You can see each other every day."

My heart sank. Because seeing Shirley every day was not what I had in mind.

"You need a stronger lock on the front door," Shirley said to me. "And more kitchen equipment. I'll buy you a blender."

"For Christ's sake!" said my father. "The one thing she doesn't need is a blender."

"And a toaster oven. For grilled sandwiches."

"Shirley," said my father, "will you leave the kid alone? This is her first apartment. Let her do things her own way."

Shirley turned in her chair to face him. "You mean you are willing to let her stay here indefinitely? Among murderers and rapists?"

"Mother . . ." I said.

"Shirley," said Leonard, "if there are murderers and rapists in this neighborhood, then they're in your neighborhood too. You better hire a body-guard."

"You are willing to let this girl live alone? At the age of seventeen?"

"Eighteen in September," I said.

My father chose not to answer her directly. "Pussycat," he said to me, "what I'm concerned with is your finances. Your mother tells me that you are running some kind of a service. Dog rescue, dog adoptions."

"Right," I said quickly, "that's absolutely right. If people lose a dog, we will find him. If people want to adopt a dog, we will provide one."

He finished his drink, and went over to the gin bottle to mix another. "So are you earning any money?"

"Of course she's not earning any money," said my mother. "She's using up her savings."

My father refreshed his drink and returned to his barber chair. "Let her speak for herself. Stop interrupting."

I got down from my barber chair and started to walk around the room. All of a sudden, I felt claustrophobic. "Look," I said to them, "I am not earning any money *yet*. But I think this is a good idea, and once it gets going it will be successful. I know it. I'm convinced of it."

"Oh, sweetie . . ." my mother began.

"Let her speak for herself!" said my father.

"I love dogs, and I want to devote my life to them. Dogs are my *raison d'être*."

"And for this you went to private school?" said my mother. "So you could live in a barbershop and work with dogs?"

"Shirley!" my father roared. "Shut up!"

To make a long story short, we got nowhere that night. My mother kept interrupting everything I said, and my father kept criticizing her for interrupting . . . and as for me, I just veered back and forth between them like a Ping-Pong ball. Shirley insisted that I could not live alone at the age of seventeen. Leonard said I *could* live alone, as long as I was self-supporting, and so we wound up nowhere.

When they left, at nine o'clock, I breathed a sigh of relief and collapsed on my bed. At least they had not dragged me back to 82nd Street kicking and screaming. At least Shirley had withdrawn, to regroup and plan her next attack.

"You know something?" I said to the four dogs, who were sitting by my bed regarding me. "Independence is exhausting."

15

Harvey and I were walking my four dogs in Central Park. It was August now, and the humidity was so thick you could have cut it with a knife. All over the borough of Manhattan, there were power failures. All over the city streets kids were opening up fire hydrants to get cool. At night the barbershop was so hot that I had to run three fans, and my refrigerator had broken down twice. But I had not gone back home.

"She's done everything but kidnap me," I said to Harvey Beaumont. "Everything but drug me and carry me home."

"It's incredible," he said, as the dogs stopped and sniffed the bushes. "I mean, you're so brave, Heidi."

I gave a bitter laugh. "Brave, I am not—but determined, yes. Because I did not go through all *this*, Harvey Beaumont, to wind up back with my mother."

"I agree with you," he said. "Completely."

Harvey was looking seedier than ever these days. My own clothes may have come from thrift shops, but they had a certain panache—whereas his garments were just plain shabby. His sneakers had holes in the toes. His jeans were patched. And his shirts were always missing buttons. He doesn't need a girlfriend, I thought, he needs a seamstress.

As we turned and headed back towards the 96th Street entrance to the Park, I cast a secret glance at him. In one way, he was rather attractive, while in another way he wasn't. But the thing he had said to me in the beginning of our relationship—about us both being too needy—was a little odd, since Harvey was still the neediest person I knew. He was forever taking my hand, or putting his arm around my shoulders, or touching my cheek—and while I didn't mind these attentions, they did reveal him to be sort of a wreck. He required mothering more than any boy I knew, and I wished that I could meet his own mother. But every time I went to the apartment, Muriel Beaumont was somewhere else—either at Miss Kamp's, or at a dog show, or giving a speech to some kennel club.

Remembering Harvey's statement that his family was comfortable, not rich, I sighed. My father has an expression that goes, "Only the rich think they're poor," so maybe that was the explanation. At a certain point of richness, one began to feel poor. What about the poor, then? The only poor friend I had ever had, Abigail Brown, had offered to give me her entire savings when—in the eighth grade— I had left the class treasury money on the subway. Abigail was poorer than anyone I knew, and on scholarship, yet she had offered me fifty bucks.

Brian was pulling on the leash like mad, so Harvey took him from me. "Heel!" said Harvey, giving the leash a jerk, and of course Brian heeled. Would anyone heel for *me*? No. It had to be Harvey.

"You know, Heidi," he said, "my mother would take Brian anytime you wanted. I've asked her about it several times."

"No thanks," I replied. "He can stay with me. Until the right person comes along."

"How can you run a dog adoption agency if you aren't willing to give the dogs away?"

"Who said I wasn't willing?"

"Heidi dear, you don't want to let any of them go."

"Happy and MacGregor are not up for adoption. They're mine."

"But Pablo and Brian aren't."

"Well," I said lamely, "I've put ads in all the papers. What else can I do?"

We were approaching Fifth Avenue, and the sky

had gone dark with impending rain. Nursemaids wheeled baby carriages along the avenue. Like us, many people were walking dogs.

And then Pablo broke loose.

I didn't see it happening, but somehow Pablo slipped his head through his new collar, and was off like a shot. I saw what he had gone after—a tabby cat, sitting in front of an apartment house—but it was already too late. Pablo was darting across Fifth Avenue, in the midst of traffic.

"Harvey!" I screamed. "Get him! He'll be killed!"

What happened next was like some kind of slapstick movie. Handing Brian over to me, Harvey took off after Pablo like an Olympic runner. Weaving in and out of the traffic, he sprinted after Pablo—who by now was chasing the cat towards Madison Avenue. A boy carrying a bag of groceries dropped them as Harvey raced by—and, excited by all the commotion, an old lady began to yell, "Stop, thief!"

Pulling the three remaining dogs with me, I hurried after Harvey and Pablo. They were crossing Madison now, the cat still ahead of them, and once again my heart faltered as I saw Pablo dodging the wheels of cars. He was so little that most of the drivers didn't see him.

Finally, in the midst of Park Avenue, Harvey made a flying tackle and brought Pablo down. The amazing thing is that he didn't squash him to death in doing so. "I've got him!" he screamed to me. "I've got him!"

By the time I had raced up to Harvey, he was on his feet and Pablo was in his arms. "Oh, God," I cried. "Thank you, Harvey."

How it happened, I do not know—but all of a sudden Harvey Beaumont and I were kissing each other. Deeply. Passionately. It startled me so much that I pulled away.

We stood there staring at each other—aware that something had happened to us. Something dangerous. And of course, this being New York, no one noticed us at all. "Harvey . . ."

"It's all right, Heidi. It's OK."

"But . . ."

He touched my cheek. "I know you don't love me. It's OK."

"You don't understand."

"I do, Heidi. Really."

We walked back towards the barbershop. In the distance, there was a low rumble of thunder. A flash of lightning lit the sky.

Once home, I gave all the dogs bowls of milk, and then I threw myself down on the bed. "God, Harvey, I thought we had lost him."

"Me too."

"Where did you learn to run like that?"

"I run every morning. At dawn. I even won the class marathon once."

He was sitting on the piano bench, watching the dogs drink their milk. He seemed very sad.

"Well, you're right about one thing," I said.

"What's that?"

"I don't want to give Brian and Pablo away. I want to keep them."

"Well . . ."

"Harvey dear, I'm supposed to be running a business. A business! My God, what I'm really running is a charity. I haven't had a single answer to my ads. And the other day I stuck flyers for Dog Rescue, Incorporated, in all the windshield wipers of all the cars on East 79th Street. Dozens and dozens of cars—and not one response. Why can't I succeed?"

"You'll succeed, Heidi. It's only a matter of time."

"Why do you have faith in me, when I don't have faith in myself?"

"Because I care about you," he said.

He was looking away from me, pretending to study one of my dog prints on the wall, an old print of some English Pointers. "Harvey?"

"Yes?"

"Harvey dear, I really and truly do *not* want to be involved with anyone right now. I'm trying to get my act together, you know?"

"Sure," he said. "I know."

"I mean, I'm very fond of you, but . . ."

"But as a friend. Right?"

I was afraid that he was going to cry—he cried so easily—so I went over and sat down next to him, on the bench. "You're a very special person, Harvey. Very talented."

"But you're just not attracted to me."

"Well . . ."

"Then how could you have kissed me that way?"

I stared at him. "I don't know."

"No one has ever kissed me that way. Ever."

Reaching out to me, he traced my lips with his fingers. His fingertips were rough, but they felt good all the same. "You're beautiful," he said.

"Oh, Harvey . . ."

"It's true. You are. You don't know it yet, but you are very very beautiful. What you've got is style."

"So do you."

"Really?"

I took his hand and held it. "Yes, really. And I think your photographs are brilliant."

"Tell that to my mother."

"Never mind her. *I* think they're brilliant, and that's all that matters right now."

"Heidi," he said, "do you think we might go to bed together? Sometime?"

It was as though he had invited me out for a pizza. Or maybe, to see a foreign film. I started to laugh. "No, Harvey, I don't think that would be a good idea. And anyway, uh, I'm a virgin."

"So am I."

I sat there for a moment, stunned. "Very few boys admit that, Harvey. Most of them tell you that they've been making out since the age of five."

"I'm different from most boys."

I squeezed his hand. "My friend, that's the understatement of the year."

16

It was two days later and Shirley was standing at my door with the following items. Three bags of groceries, a new shower head, an electric coffeepot, and a white chenille bedspread. "I came over in a cab," she explained. "There was no other way."

"Mom," I sighed, "what is all this stuff? You're acting like the Red Cross."

"Well, you could do worse," she said, as she marched past me with her bundles. *"Some* girls have no one to look after them. You, at least, have me."

All four dogs jumped up on her—and angrily, she pushed them away. "It smells like a kennel in here, Heidi. It's awful."

"Then why do you keep coming over?"

"Because I'm your mother. And I can't stand to see you living this way. No food in the refrigerator, dog bowls all over the floor. And if I have to look at that rumpled bed once more, I'll go mad. So I bought you a pretty bedspread. At Bloomingdale's."

"But you've already bought me so much."

"Nonsense," she replied. "You need everything."

Shirley had been making these trips to the barber-shop since the second week in July. She had brought me kitchen equipment, bathroom equipment, scented soaps from Saks Fifth Avenue, new towels, and a Waring blender. I had refused her offer of an electric toaster oven, and I had also refused to accept the home hair drier she had offered to buy me. Home hair drier? I had a crew cut—it dried in three minutes.

"This kitchen is filthy!" she called to me from the back of the shop. "What am I supposed to do, Heidi? Get you a maid? Why can't you clean up after yourself?"

"I've been *busy*," I called back to her.

As she bustled around in the kitchen, I sat on the edge of my bed, thinking about Harvey. He was never out of my thoughts these days, and I couldn't figure out why. I mean, I was *not* in love with Harvey Beaumont the Third, and his implication that he was in love with me was hard to accept. He was simply on the rebound—though I had to admit that four years was stretching it a bit. Only Harvey Beaumont, I decided, could carry a torch for someone for four years.

"Your milk's gone sour!" Shirley called from the

kitchen. "Does this refrigerator work, or what?"

I turned to MacGregor, who was sitting on my bed perusing me. "This is not exactly the way to leave home, is it MacGregor?"

His ears pricked up and he gave me one of his intelligent looks, one of his glances that is almost human. "Look," said the glance, "what can you do? She's your mother."

Shirley marched out of the kitchen, an apron over her print dress, a dish towel in her hand. "I'm washing up those dishes for you. There isn't a clean dish in the house."

"Mom . . ."

"And after that, I'll tackle the refrigerator. It smells."

She marched away again — an army of one — and I was left sitting there with MacGregor. The other three dogs had conked out on the floor. "Actually," I said to MacGregor, "I didn't leave home at all. I just brought it with me."

I lay back on the unmade bed and closed my eyes. On September 15th I would be eighteen, and I was looking forward to it like it was the beginning of the world. . . . The thing that was so surprising these days was my father's attitude towards me. The other day he had phoned and we had talked for an hour. "I thought you were really mad at me," I'd said to him. "About college."

"What I figure is this," he said. "You'll get a little life experience now, and go to college later. Lots of people do that. It's done all the time."

"Well . . ."

"At least keep an open mind, pussycat. That's all I ask."

"OK, Daddy, I will."

There was a pause, and then he said, "I'm proud of you, you know."

"What?"

"I said, I'm proud of you. The way you're trying to function on your own. All I've ever wanted for you, baby, is that you should be independent."

"Right."

"Because your *mother* is so dependent that she can't even hail a cab alone. How she went through Europe this summer, I do not understand."

"Well, as I told you, they didn't have too wonderful a time."

"The point is that you've tried to strike out on your own, and I think that's good. In a year or so, you'll go to college."

"OK," I said. "Let's leave it open."

I heard him clear his throat on the other end of the phone, and then he said, "Baby, there's something I want to tell you."

120

Here it comes, I thought. He's going to tell me about his new girlfriend. "Yes?" I said.

"Sweetie, you know that you and I don't keep secrets from each other. At least, not very often. So I wanted to tell you that I've met a young lady I like very much. We're going out together."

"No kidding," I said, trying to sound surprised. "Gee. I'm glad for you."

"Her name is Eden Warburg, and she runs a bookstore on MacDougal Street. She's a very interesting person."

"Right."

"And because you're a grown-up girl now, I want to tell you that Eden and I have been going away every weekend. To Shelter Island. I think you're old enough for me to tell you that."

"Well, sure," I said. "Of course."

But for some reason, my heart had sunk down to my boots. Don't ask me why—but the idea of Leonard having another affair depressed the hell out of me. First Jane Anne Mosley, the writer—and now Eden Warburg, the bookseller. It was a bit too much.

"She's a very lovely person," Leonard was saying, "and I want us all to have lunch very soon. I know you'll like her, Heidi. She has great class."

"What kind of bookstore does she run?"

"Metaphysical books. Psychic phenomena, and things like that. Reincarnation."

"I see."

"She's got an M.A. from Columbia."

"How do you get to Shelter Island on the weekends? It's so far away."

Leonard gave a guilty laugh. "We take the commuter plane to East Hampton, and then we drive. I leave my car at the airport."

"Oh," I said. "Right."

But after we hung up, I just sat there—trying to imagine my father having an affair with a woman who ran a metaphysical bookstore. Poor Leonard. He has always been so intellectually starved that he is a pushover for people who seem educated. And here was Eden Warburg, from Columbia University. Eden! How the hell had she gotten a name like that?

My mother spent most of that afternoon cleaning up my kitchen, and the minute she was gone, I took the four dogs for a long walk by the East River. When we returned home, I noticed that someone had slipped a letter under my door.

I retrieved it and took it inside. And, after liberating the dogs from their leashes, I sat down to read my mysterious letter. It was from Harvey. "My dearest Heidi," it began.

My dearest Heidi,

I'm writing this because I don't know how to face you with the news that I think we should part. I care for you terribly, and know that you don't care for me, and so why, basically, should we go on? I feel that the way I moon around is a burden to you — and it hurts my pride to behave so stupidly, and yet I don't seem to be able to pull myself together. Whenever I see you, I fall apart a little — because I think you are wonderful and because I love you so much. There. I've said it. I love you. Heidi, please remember me with happiness because we've had good times together. I have more fun with you than anybody, and that's the part that is hard to let go of. Heidi, good-bye.

Harvey

17

Harvey's letter had a strange effect on me, and I couldn't figure it out. My first feeling was anger, and then I just felt relieved — like a burden had been lifted. But as the days went on, and as Harvey's absence became more tangible, I began to miss him. It was like my left foot had been removed, or something. As though a part of my self was gone.

How could this be? I did not love him, and yet his absence was causing me such pain that it became physical. Yes, Harvey's absence gave me a stomachache, and then a toothache, and then it became a plain old heartache. So I allowed four days to pass, and then I decided to confront him. It was terrible, having him gone, and the dogs missed him too.

I picked up the phone to call him a dozen times, and put the phone down. I wrote him letters and tore them up. In one of these letters I said, "You better get over here pronto, because MacGregor misses you so much he has lost his appetite."

Which was true. MacGregor had suddenly stopped eating and lay in the barbershop staring at the front door.

Finally, on the fifth day, I decided that I would go to the Beaumont apartment and have the whole thing out with him. I would appear that very morning and ask Harvey to explain himself. "Because," I said to the dogs, "this situation is both silly and artificial. I miss him, and I know he misses me, so what is the point? He's the best friend I've ever had."

At nine that morning I was standing outside the Beaumonts' front door, with a photo magazine I had bought Harvey days ago. Nervous is too mild a word for the way I felt, and the knowledge that I would have to explain my presence to Holmes, the butler, worried me. Suppose he said that the Beaumonts never received unexpected guests? Suppose he said that "Master Harvey" was otherwise engaged?

I took a deep breath and rang the doorbell. No one answered.

I rang again, and finally the door was flung open by a smallish woman wearing whipcord pants and a blue shirt. She had red hair, and angry green eyes, and I had the terrible feeling she was Harvey's mother. "Yes?" she said coldly. "May I help you?"

"Uh, good morning," I said. "I'm Heidi Rosenbloom. A friend of Harvey's."

"Harvey?" she said, as though the name was not quite familiar.

"Uh, yes ma'am. I'm sorry to bother you at this hour—but I thought Holmes would answer the door."

"This is Holmes' day off. I am Harvey's mother."

"Yes, ma'am. I figured you were."

And then there was a pause.

The woman gazed at me as though I had two heads. "What did you say your name was, dear? Your last name, I mean."

"Rosenbloom."

"Ah," she said. "I see."

What I *should* have said was that my name was Finklestein. Epstein, Horowitz, Katz and Goldberg. Lowenthal and Kaplan. Schwartz. Because it was all too clear that this woman was not used to entertaining people with ethnic names. For one second, I heard my father telling me, long ago, that I hadn't the slightest idea of what anti-Semitism was like. Wrong. Now I knew.

"Rosenbloom," I repeated. "It's a Jewish name."

"Won't you come in?" she said stiffly. "Perhaps I can help you."

She ushered me into the foyer, but no farther.

126

Because it was obvious that people with the name of Rosenbloom were kept in the hall. Steady, I said to myself. Keep a lid on your temper. This dame isn't worth it.

She was around a size twelve, and not very tall — but her features were perfect, and her short red hair was luxuriant. I am not a connoisseur of clothes, but I knew that hers were expensive. Hell. I had known women like her before, because many of my classmates at Spencer had mothers like that. Only *their* mothers were not unpleasant.

"So," said Muriel Beaumont. "What can I do for you?"

"I need to see Harvey. Is he home?"

She shook her head. "I'm afraid not. He's gone up to Connecticut, to visit his father."

I felt a pang of disappointment. "How long will he be away?"

She looked surprised, as though I had asked a very personal question. "I really don't know."

It was uncomfortable, just standing there in the hall, but since it was clear that this interview was going to be conducted vertically, I said, "I'm the girl with the Irish Setter named Brian. I think Harvey has mentioned me to you."

"Ah, yes," she replied, "the Setter. Did you find him a home?"

"Not yet."

"Harvey tells me that he's a very good dog. Good conformation."

"Yes. He is."

"Well, if you can't place him, he's always welcome here."

Which is more than I am, I thought. Aloud, I said, "I brought Harvey this photo magazine. It's got an article in it on macro, and some of the pictures look like his."

Muriel Beaumont took the magazine from me and leafed through it. "Hmmm," she said, "interesting. But of course, these are professional pictures. Harvey's just an amateur."

I felt anger rising in me, but tried to keep it down. "Oh, I don't know. I think he's pretty good."

"You're a photographer?"

"No, ma'am, I'm not. But I do think he's talented. Actually, I admire Harvey very much."

She laughed, and it was such a bitter laugh that it caught me up short. "Well, good for you," she said. "Good for you."

"I gather that you don't like his pictures."

She shrugged. "It's just a phase, like all the others. When he was little, he wanted to be a ballet dancer. Can you believe it? And then he decided that he wanted to be a writer. *Now* it's photography, and next year I'm sure it will be something else. The trouble, of course, is that his father indulges him in all this, but there's nothing I can do about it."

"No, ma'am."

"Frankly, I find the idea of photographing decaying vegetables rather disgusting. Have you been in his room? It smells like a Puerto Rican grocery store."

"I've been in his room several times. It smelled fine."

It was clear to me that she wanted me to go, so I walked towards the door. "Well, it's been nice meeting you," I said. "I'll try Harvey again in a few days."

"I wouldn't, if I were you. He may be gone for some time."

"Then just tell him Heidi Rosenbloom dropped by. *Rosenbloom*, with two o's."

By the time I hit the street, I was so angry that I was almost seeing double. No wonder Harvey Beaumont the Third had all the confidence of a dying albatross. That woman would be enough to destroy anyone. My classmate Peter Applebaum, not known for his subtlety, would call her a ballbreaker. Wow. No wonder Harvey was the way he was. No wonder the father lived in Connecticut.

For the rest of that day—as I walked my dogs,

and placed newspaper ads, and shopped for groceries—I thought about Muriel Beaumont. Harvey had told me that she had had a very strange life, that she had grown up in boarding schools and had little contact with her parents, but did that excuse such awful behavior? For the first time in many years, I felt grateful for Shirley. Yes, she was eccentric, and God knows she was pushy. But at least—at least!—she loved me.

18

Harvey had said that he ran every morning at dawn. So what I decided to do was wait outside his building every single morning until he returned from Connecticut. I have to admit to you that it was not exactly easy to rise at four, feed and walk the dogs, get them back to the shop, and then hurry over to Fifth Avenue. But I did it. I did it every morning for five days, and it paid off.

I was standing across from his apartment building in the dim light, a sort of apple-green light that seemed ominous, and it was around five thirty A.M. Fifth Avenue was almost deserted, and the only people out of doors were joggers. Harvey, I said in the privacy of my mind, *please appear*.

And that's just what he did. Sprinting through the front door of his building, he suddenly came into view and took off like a shot. He was wearing a pair of white shorts, and a white T-shirt, and white jogging shoes.

It all happened so quickly that for a moment I

131

didn't react. Then I took off after him. But my God, he ran fast! He was like a white streak, going down Fifth Avenue, a kind of wind.

Undaunted, I hurried after him until we reached 70th Street. People were starting to walk their dogs, and the apple-green sky was growing dark, as though it might rain. It had been raining all summer, and before that it had rained all spring. Maybe Shirley is right, I thought irrelevantly. Maybe atomic testing has ruined our weather.

Abruptly, Harvey stopped and studied his watch. I assumed that he wanted to see how long it had taken him to run twelve blocks. As for me, I was so winded that I could hardly speak. "Harvey," I gasped. "It's me."

He didn't hear me, so I staggered up to him and took him by the arm. "Harvey. It's me. Hi."

He jumped back, as though he couldn't believe his eyes. "Heidi, you startled me! What are you doing here?"

"I've been waiting for you for *days* in front of your building. Waiting for you to come out."

"Really?"

"Yes, really. And there's no one else in the world I would do that for. Where have you *been*? Why didn't you write me? How could you disappear like that?"

132

To my amazement, I felt tears coming down my face—and then we were in each other's arms. "You are just so weird," I said to him. "So utterly . . ."

But we were kissing now, and there was nothing in the universe that could have stopped us. And not only was *I* crying, but he was crying too. It was like a scene from a soap opera.

"Harvey . . ."

"Sh," he said. "It will be all right, Heidi. Everything will be all right."

"But . . ."

"I love you so much."

"I love you too."

We pulled back and stared at each other. It was true. I loved him. And I hadn't even known it.

"You . . . love me?" he said slowly.

"Yes, I do. But I didn't recognize it. You know?"

"Yes. Sure."

"I thought love was something else. Something unreal. But this is so real it's almost killing me. . . . Harvey, you're so strange. I never know what to make of you."

"You're strange too, Heidi."

"I am?"

"That's why we like each other. We're two odd-balls."

He took my hand and led me over to a bench

133

on the sidewalk, and we sat there holding hands. He leaned over and kissed me again, and I clung to him. "Where have you been all this time, Harvey?"

"At the farm in Connecticut. At Dad's. He was wonderful. I mean, he didn't ask questions or anything. He just let me play around with the camera. I photographed his garden."

"When you say farm, do you mean a working farm?"

"No, no, it's just an old farmhouse that he and Mother bought long ago. It's renovated, of course, and very nice. Dad's passion is birds."

"Birdwatching?"

"Right. He knows everything about birds you can imagine."

"He sounds very solitary."

Harvey smiled. "He is. Like me."

I smiled back at him. "Would you let me wreck your solitude? For a little while?"

He kissed me — a long, deep kiss. "Yes."

"Let's go back to the shop. MacGregor's missed you so much that he's starving himself."

We walked back to the barbershop holding hands, and it was like the entire world had changed. People on the street looked kind, and the green sky looked beautiful, and even the thick, humid heat felt comforting. The world had changed, and Harvey Beaumont was no longer a very short boy who looked fifteen and talked like an elderly stockbroker. Who he *was*, I did not know. But I intended to find out.

"Has anyone been responding to the ads?" he asked, as we strolled along.

"No. Or rather, yes. In the last few days I've had five phone calls—two of them pornographic, and the other three crazy. I mean, a woman called to ask if I would adopt a pony. And then another woman called to ask me to find her Poodle who disappeared five years ago. In Brooklyn."

"It will get better. You'll see."

I stopped on the sidewalk and gazed at him. "Harvey, for a pessimist, you're the most optimistic person I know."

19

MacGregor went crazy when he saw Harvey, and so did the other dogs. They were all over him, kissing him, jumping up on him—and eventually he had had enough. *"Down,"* he said. And, by God, every one of them sat down.

I made us both some coffee and brought out a box of donuts. "Harvey . . ." I said tentatively.

"Yes?" he replied. "What?"

"How could I have loved you all this time and not known it?"

He bit into his donut. "You said it yourself—because you thought love was something unreal. Like an old Garbo film or something."

"Do you like Greta Garbo?"

"Oh, yes. I always watch her films on TV."

"So does my mother. She's got a thing about her. . . . Oh listen! I met *your* mother. Just the other day."

Beneath his tan, Harvey seemed to go pale. "You did?"

"I dropped in at the apartment, looking for you, and she answered the door. We chatted for a while."

"God," said Harvey.

"We had quite a little talk."

His lips tightened. "I bet you did. She's difficult, isn't she?"

I hesitated, not sure what I should say. "Well yes — she is a bit difficult. But that's probably because she's so tense."

"She's always been that way. She's so tense she gives herself headaches."

"Really?"

"Don't get me wrong, Heidi, in many ways she's a wonderful person. And a genius with dogs. When she used to show her dogs at Madison Square Garden, people would crowd the bleachers to watch. And the obedience trials! You should have seen her in those days, taking her dogs through their paces. They used to put her photo in *The Times*. On the sports page."

I finished my donut and took a sip of coffee. "Harvey, I'm afraid this is going to shock you — but I don't think you should be living with her."

He glanced up. "Really? Then where should I be living?"

"Here. With me."

He looked so stunned that for a moment I wanted

to take the words back. I mean, he looked like I had hit him over the head with a hammer. "You mean . . ." he said, "that you'd like me to live with you?"

"Yes. Here in the shop."

"And be your lover?"

I looked him straight in the eye. "Yes."

"God," he said.

"Don't make your decision right away. Think it over for a while. But I think we'd be good together. And the dogs really like you."

It was not the dialogue I had imagined for my first love affair, but what the hell. Because not only is life the thing that happens while you are making other plans—love is the thing that happens too. While you are telling yourself that you are not in love at all.

Harvey took my hand and turned it over. And then he kissed the palm. And suddenly I knew that he would be a very good lover, and that I wanted to go to bed with him. "Is it a bad thing that we're both virgins?" I asked.

He blushed. "No, I don't think it's bad at all. Because . . . it will be a new thing for both of us."

"You're right."

We were sitting side by side on the bed, and

his face was still the color of a beet. "Actually," he said, "many of the sex manuals I've read *recommend* virginity. In the old days, of course, people used to jump into bed with anyone. But now, in the light of certain . . ."

Afraid that this was going to turn into a philosophical debate, I kissed him. Then I pulled his T-shirt over his head and rumpled his bangs. He pulled me down with him and we started kissing . . . and then I lost track of the time. It was just his body and my body, together. The two of us together for the very first time. And it was perfect.

20

I woke up at two that afternoon, yawned, and realized that Harvey was with me. He slept quietly on his back, a little smile on his face—and very gently, I leaned over and patted him. The dogs were shut up in the kitchen and they were whimpering.

"OK," I muttered. "OK, dogs. Hold your horses."

I pulled a shirt on over my nakedness and released the four dogs, who bounded joyfully into the front room. Wakened by the commotion, Harvey sat up in bed.

"I have to walk them," I said. "They're going crazy."

He could not look at me. I mean, he was so filled with emotion that he just stared at the floor. Wrapping the sheet around him, he staggered to the bathroom. In a few minutes he was back in bed, his face pressed into the pillow.

I sat down next to him. "I have to walk the dogs. Will you make some coffee while I'm gone?"

"Yes," he said in a muffled voice. "Sure."

"Make some sandwiches, too."

"Right."

"Are you OK, Harvey?"

"Mmmm," said the muffled voice.

I kissed his hair. "I know how you feel. Because I feel the same way."

Suddenly I remembered that this was the day that I was supposed to send Veronica a telegram. "I'll be back in a half hour," I said. *"Au revoir."*

A few minutes later, walking the dogs down First Avenue, I realized that I was no longer alone. I, Heidi, America's greatest loner, was now connected to another human being. How could people take love lightly? Or even, throw it away? To be in love with another person, to be connected to him, was the most miraculous thing in the world.

Since Pablo could not keep up with the other dogs, I let him pee and then I tucked him under my arm, oblivious to the comments of a male passerby who said, "Hey kiddo, what's that under your arm? A cockroach?" Then I stopped at a phone booth and called Western Union. Giving them my name and phone number, I sent Veronica the following message: "It happened. Not boring. Beautiful. Love, Heidi."

At four o'clock, Harvey was still with me, and I wondered if his mother had missed him yet. He had been gone since five thirty that morning. Lying in his arms, as the dogs dozed on the floor, I said, "Harvey dear, will your mother be missing you? It's getting late."

"No, no," he said softly. "It's all right. She never knows what I do."

"That's not the impression *I* got. I felt that she was very possessive where you're concerned."

He kissed my cheek. "She's possessive, all right, but at the same time she has always ignored me. I was really raised by Holmes. And a couple of governesses."

"Poor baby," I said, hugging him tighter. "What an awful childhood."

"Oh, I don't know. Chandler always thought it was great material—if one was going to be a writer, that is. I would go around to all these dog shows with Mother and Miss Kamp, and Mother would show her Setters. She was well known in those days, and people would say to me, 'She's *your* mother? You're a lucky boy.' It was like having a celebrity for a mother. People would ask for her autograph."

Right, I thought to myself, but it wiped you off the blackboard. Because Muriel Beaumont is a lady who does not like competition. And that's why she takes you down and belittles you. She needs to be the star. "Why does she have such a passion for dogs?" I said aloud. "Why not people?"

Harvey laughed. "You are hardly the person to be asking that question."

"I know, I know, but I do like people. Your mother doesn't like them at all."

He drew away from me. "I think it's because . . . because she doesn't feel lovable. No one, with the exception of Dad, ever really loved her."

I pulled Harvey back down on the pillow. "Harvey Beaumont," I said, "here we are, in love, and do you know something? It's only sheer luck that we ever got together. Suppose I had taken your farewell letter for real? Suppose I hadn't come to find you?"

He smiled, a secret little smile that I had never seen before. "There's an old saying—if you love something, set it free. If it comes back to you, it's yours."

"Wow. Where did you find that? It's very good."

"Some book, somewhere. I do so much reading."

"It's funny that you love me, Harvey. Because intellectual, I am not."

He took my face between his hands and kissed me. "I don't want an intellectual. I want a lover. A true love."

"For always?"

"Yes. For always."

We held on tight to each other, and I couldn't believe my luck—my sheer good fortune in finding someone as sweet and gentle as Harvey Beaumont the Third. He would never be unfaithful to me, or betray me, and the next thing on his mind would probably be marriage. No, I said to myself, live with him first. Veronica says that marriage spoils everything—and she should know. Her mother's been married three times.

At six P.M., I finally persuaded Harvey to go home. I needed to be alone for a while, to think about what had happened to us. I needed some solitude. But no sooner had he left—wearing his white T-shirt and white shorts—than Shirley barged in. She didn't knock, she didn't buzz, she just barreled her way in, carrying some sort of machine. "The door was open," she announced cheerfully, "so I came in. And baby, wait till you see what I brought you."

What she had brought me was an electric lettuce drier, a machine into which you stick wet lettuce before you place it in a salad. "Mom . . ."

"Not a word!" she said. "I have one of these myself, and it's the most useful thing I've ever owned."

She bustled back to the kitchen, to place the

electric lettuce drier on the shelf, and then she returned to the front room. "What about a movie tonight, Heidi? There's a good one playing over at the Criterion. On Lexington."

She was sitting on my piano bench, trying to keep the dogs from jumping on her. "Down," she kept saying. "No! Down, I say."

I sat down on the wooden chair, facing her. "Mom . . ."

"Do you know that your bed is still unmade? At six in the evening?"

"Mom," I said more firmly. "I have something to ask you."

"Oh?" she said, pushing at Happy, who was sniffing her shoes.

"It's this way. I have to ask you not to drop in on me anymore. It just isn't right."

She looked as if I had slapped her. "Not drop in on you? I'm your mother."

"Yes," I said, "you are. But that doesn't mean that I don't need privacy."

Her eyes narrowed. "And why, may I ask, do you suddenly need privacy?"

"Because I have a boyfriend. His name is Harvey and sometimes he'll be sleeping over. Actually, I've asked him to come and live here."

Shirley clutched at her throat—a gesture straight

out of a Dracula movie we had both seen recently. "A boyfriend!" she exclaimed.

All of a sudden, I wanted to laugh. I just wanted to break into wild, crazy, hysterical laughter. Because for *years* she had been asking me why there were no boys in my life—and now that there was one, she was shocked. "I thought you'd be pleased," I said.

"Pleased! My God, Heidi, what's happened to you? First you leave home, and then you tell me you're having an affair. And you expect me to be calm?"

"Didn't you have an affair with Dr. Eisenberg? Last year?"

A pause here, to explain that exactly one year ago Shirley had gone out with a foot doctor named Emmanuel Eisenberg. He was a complete and total bore, and eventually she broke up with him. But I knew they had had an affair. At his apartment on Park Avenue. At his Long Island house.

"Dr. Eisenberg is none of your business," she said stiffly. "And anyway, I haven't seen him for a year."

"But you did have an affair."

She gave me a sharp look. "Heidi, I am a middle-aged woman, whereas you are seventeen. My God, before I married your father I hadn't even necked with a boy. A good-night kiss was all they got, at the front door."

"Maybe that wasn't such a good thing."

"Don't you be fresh with me, Heidi! Seventeen — or eighteen — is much too young for these things."

"What things?"

"For sex!" she screamed. "What boy will ever marry you if you throw yourself away like this? Who will be interested?"

"Mom, the world has changed. Women don't need to use virginity as a bargaining chip anymore. Women are gaining the same rights as men."

"Rights!" she said in disgust. "What good are rights, if you can't interest a man? And men are just not interested in girls who have slept around. I know what I'm talking about, Heidi, take my word."

But she *didn't* know what she was talking about, and somehow this made me very sad. She was as wrong about this subject as she was about everything else — as wrong about my sex life as she was about my need for kitchen equipment. "I'm sorry," I said. "But you'll have to phone me before you come over."

She straightened her silk dress and walked towards the door. "I'm phoning your father," she said, "because things have gotten completely out of hand here. I knew if we let you live alone something terrible would happen. And it has, Heidi. It has!"

21

What more can I tell you about that crazy summer? Harvey moved in with me, and his mother went wild. Shirley came over to meet Harvey, and *she* went wild. Then Leonard, aroused by Shirley's alarms, arrived one evening — unannounced — to see what the hell was going on. He marched into the barbershop like the whole United States Army rolled into one, but the minute he saw Harvey he faltered. Obviously, Harvey Beaumont the Third, with his blond bangs, was not what he expected.

"Look," he said to Shirley over the phone the next day, "as usual, you exaggerated. I mean, I go over there, expecting to find her living with a truck driver, and I find a little boy. He's a *child*, Shirley, and as shy as a little mouse. And he comes from a good family. The father's a banker."

I had come over to Shirley's place to get an old raincoat of mine — and I was listening on the hall extension. A crummy thing to do, of course, but very instructive.

"He's eighteen years old," Shirley said to Leonard. "He only looks young."

"A nice kid. And lovely manners. He went to The Lawrence School For Boys."

"He photographs vegetables," Shirley said angrily. "Closeups of vegetables."

"So what, for God's sake?"

"*He* photographs vegetables, and *she* rescues stray dogs. It's nutty."

"You know something?" said Leonard. "I visit with them for about an hour, and then, when I'm leaving, he walks me to the door. And in a very low voice, he tells me that he loves her and wants to marry her. It was very sweet."

"You mean you approve of this situation!" Shirley screamed into the phone. "I don't believe what I'm hearing!"

"Shirley," said my father, "she could do worse. Believe me, she could do much much worse."

Back to that famous evening for a minute. As I said, Leonard had marched through the front door like an army of one, but then Harvey had disarmed him. I mean, Harvey had made him a drink, and rushed to get him an ashtray, and he had been so polite that Leonard had been nonplussed. So, instead of kicking Harvey out of the place, he had wound up talking to us about commitment, and responsibility — and birth control. *That* one we could have done without, but Leonard felt it important to discuss the use of birth control by unmarried people. Poor Harvey sat there listening to this, his face as red as a beet, and I was pretty miserable myself. Because of course we were taking all the usual precautions. "So this is the way I feel," my father had said. "You two want to behave like grown-up people. OK. Very good. But with adulthood comes responsibility."

Yes yes, we had said. Right, we had agreed. And finally, Leonard had left. But the turn the evening had taken rocked me. I was living with a boy, and my father approved. Fantastic.

Muriel Beaumont came over, saw the barbershop, and was stunned. But there was nothing she could do about it. Harvey was eighteen, and in a few weeks I would be too. Then Harvey's father phoned us — Harvey was out at the time — and said that he was looking forward to meeting me. He sounded very elderly and very kind. And he also sounded like the name Rosenbloom was not a threat to his mental health. "Rosenbloom," he mused. "I knew a Bob Rosenbloom once. In publishing."

As my birthday approached, Harvey and I began

to work things out. I mean, in bed we were perfect—but out of bed we had a few small problems. Such as the fact that I was messy and he was neat. Such as the fact that his photo equipment took up a lot of room. And such as the fact that it really was hard for us to live with four dogs. Harvey had not only brought his photo equipment to the shop, but all of his books and records. It was getting crowded.

Then—of all things—Dog Rescue, Incorporated, received its first genuine phone call.

Harvey was out at the time, doing our grocery shopping, when the phone rang. "Is this the dog rescue organization?" a woman's voice said.

"Uh, yes," I said cautiously. "May I help you?"

"I just saw your ad in *The Village Voice*. On the Chihuahua. We'd like to adopt him."

"You would?" I said, surprised at how shaky my voice sounded.

"Yes, we really would. *Our* Chihuahua just died, and the children are heartbroken. We live in Gramercy Park."

"This Chihuahua is very old," I said to her. "I'm not sure if you'd like him."

"That doesn't matter at all."

"Why not get a puppy?"

"Because we don't want to have to train a puppy."

"Well, actually, this dog doesn't have the best disposition in the world. He can be cranky."

The woman was beginning to sound annoyed. "Your ad in *The Voice* said that if we needed a dog, you would provide one. Is that true or not?"

"Well, yes. It's true."

"What's your adoption fee?"

"Twenty-five dollars."

"That will be fine," said the woman. "May I have your address?"

To make a long story short, Pablo was adopted that evening—into a kind, loving family composed of two parents and two little girls. They were nice people. And one of the girls picked up Pablo and hugged him the minute they were introduced. It was a good home for Pablo—Gramercy Park—but the minute they were out of the door, I began to cry. It was like losing a child. A foster child.

"Darling," said Harvey, "be glad for him. He's gone to a wonderful home. And they didn't even mind that he was old."

"I know," I sobbed, "but I loved that little runt. I really did."

Harvey sat on the bed and pulled me down on his lap. "Heidi, dearest, the point is to get the dogs adopted. Not to keep them."

153

"I know," I sobbed. "I know."

"Heidi, dearest, everything will be all right. I promise you."

And suddenly I believed him. Things *would* be all right, and I *would* learn to give my foster dogs away—and someday Harvey's mother, and my mother, would see that Harvey and I were meant for each other. Harvey would enroll at the Manhattan Institute of Photography—a new plan of his—and I, to please Leonard, would start taking a few courses at Hunter College. We would find Brian a home, and reorganize the barbershop, and if they ever demolished the building . . . well, then we would move on. Because the point of the whole thing was that Harvey Beaumont and I had found each other. But you know something? I was beginning to realize that love didn't have to be something you drowned in. I mean, I was born independent, and independent I would remain. My English teacher Mr. Moss had once read us a quotation from Rilke which said that lovers should be the guardians of each other's solitude—and it was the best quotation I knew. Harvey Beaumont and I would protect each other's solitude. And each of us, in separate ways, would grow up.

"Harvey," I said, staring at him, "the most amazing thing has happened."

"Oh?" he said, stroking my cheek. "What's that, dearest?"

"You no longer look like Truman Capote. I mean it, Harvey. All of a sudden you don't."

And then we both began to laugh.